Gateway To Doom

TOM SWIFT®
GATEWAY TO DOOM
VICTOR APPLETON

Wanderer Books
Published by Simon & Schuster, New York

Published by WANDERER BOOKS
A Simon & Schuster Division of
Gulf & Western Corporation
Simon & Schuster Building
1230 Avenue of the Americas
New York, New York 10020
Manufactured in the United States of America
10   9   8   7   6   5   4   3   2   1

WANDERER and colophon are trademarks
of Simon & Schuster

TOM SWIFT is a trademark of Stratemeyer Syndicate,
registered in the United States Patent and Trademark Office

Library of Congress Cataloging in Publication Data

Appleton, Victor, pseud.
Gateway to doom.

(Tom Swift/Victor Appleton; #9)
Summary: Tom Swift, aboard the science survey ship
"Hawking," discovers unusual sunspot activity indicating
the sun will soon explode, destroying all life in the
solar system.
[1. Science fiction] I. Title. II. Series: Apple-
ton, Victor, pseud. Tom Swift; no. 9
PZ7.A652Gat   1983   [Fic]   82-20238
ISBN 0-671-43956-1
ISBN 0-671-43957-X (pbk.)

CONTENTS

Chapter One

Tom Swift was peering into the eyepiece of the telescope aboard the science survey ship *Hawking* trying to find the location of a black hole. This "hole in space" was a miniature singularity, tinier than a grain of sand. In spite of its smallness, it possessed an incredibly powerful gravitational pull and sucked in any debris around it like a vacuum cleaner.

Suddenly there was a tremendous explosion. Its intense white light almost blinded Tom. He jumped away from the eyepiece, tears caused by the brilliant flare flowing down his cheek. Tiny bright yellow and blue spots danced in front of his eyes.

"Wow!" he exclaimed. "Wonder what that could have been?"

He turned in the bucket seat and made sure his elbows didn't hit any of the instruments in the cramped cockpit. Fiddling with the radio dial, he spun it until he picked up the crackle of solar flare–induced interference—and a faint cry for help.

"Mayday," came the weak signal. "Engines blown. Solar flare destroyed control circuits. A-drift. Mayday. Mayday!"

"This is science ship *Hawking*," Tom radioed back. "Identify and give location. I think I saw your engines explode. I'm not far away."

The static caused by the solar prominences arching up from the turbulent face of the Sun drowned out his message. He repeated it, then listened for a response. It came quickly.

"Cargo ship *Ponderous*," said the voice, barely audible over the interference. "Am turning on homing beacon, standard frequency. Please help me. I'm in bad shape! Ship's losing air!"

"On my way," Tom said, lining up the *Hawking* with the steady beep-beep of the emergency homing device carried by all ships. He fastened the buckles of his seat belt around his big-boned, six-foot frame, pushed a lock of sandy blond hair out of his eyes, then confidently went to work at the control board. His deft fingers found the right buttons. The onboard computer hummed as it calculated the vectors required to match velocities with the other ship, and then Tom felt the sudden kick of acceleration.

He was right on target. In less than ten minutes he visually located the disabled cargo vessel. A sure touch on the controls brought the *Hawking* around so that both ships were side by side. Even though they traveled several miles a second through space, they hung together as if they were standing still. Both were moving at exactly the same speed and in the same direction.

Tom tried to communicate with the pilot of the *Ponderous*, but failed. The static was so bad that the radio was practically useless. He unbuckled his seat belt and peered out the inch-thick glassite porthole. The cargo ship was less than a hundred yards away, seemingly dead in space.

"Come in, *Ponderous*," Tom tried again.

No response.

"This solar flare's getting dangerous," he said aloud to himself, checking several meters and noting the high readings. "That guy's going to be cooked if he doesn't leave right now."

Luckily, Tom was well-protected inside the science ship. While he hadn't intended to be deluged by more than the usual amount of cosmic radiation as he studied the vagrant black hole, the *Hawking* had recently been used for close studies of the Sun and was still equipped with lead shields.

"Come in, over," he tried once more.

Realizing the static was too fierce for any communication, he flipped off the radio. He spun in his chair and wheeled the telescope into position. Studying the cargo ship with it proved to be more difficult than he'd anticipated. The telescope was perfect for star gazing and detecting minute movements at great distances, but up close it was completely out of focus.

In disgust, Tom Swift swung away and pulled himself out of the chair. He didn't like feeling helpless and he had to know what was going on. He was active and had an inquiring mind. That was one reason why he was alone in space investigating the black hole. Scientific knowledge aside, he had to be doing something, and things had become rather dull since he and his friends had retrieved the stolen *SeaGlobe* in *Ark Two*.

Tom snapped on his helmet, spinning it in the bayonet mountings until it clicked. If the pilot wasn't coming to him, Tom would go to the pilot. Even though only a short time had elapsed between the distress call and Tom's arrival, he knew that the spatial atmosphere was filled with radiation deadly enough to severely injure anyone who was unprotected.

He doubted that the pilot aboard the *Ponderous* had any radiation shielding at all.

Tom hesitated when the airlock cycled open. Only a hundred yards separated him from the cargo ship, but it was millions of light years beyond—if he missed his target. He knew that he wouldn't have enough velocity to leave the Solar System, that if he couldn't reach the cargo ship he would remain a tiny planetoid circling the Sun. The distance to the stars looked so vast it gave him a momentary pang of fear.

He pushed it out of his mind. A man's life was in jeopardy. He couldn't let hesitant thoughts get in his way. His strong legs pushed against the airlock frame, and he hurled himself away from the security of the *Hawking*.

"Hang on," he said quietly, as if to assure himself as well as the trapped man. "Just hang in there and everything will be fine."

He performed an adroit somersault that brought his feet up to where his head had been. He touched down lightly on the cargo ship's hull. Not wanting to be exposed any longer to the radiation invisibly surging around him, he hastened to open the airlock and duck inside.

Even a small bit of metal between him and the

solar flare was better than nothing.

He awkwardly moved down a narrow, low-ceilinged corridor toward the control room. There he found the pilot, slumped against the bulkhead.

"Are you all right?" Tom asked anxiously. He knelt down and examined the man. The pilot was semiconscious, his eyes heavily lidded and his lips moving in weak response. "You've got to get moving," Tom cried, then realized his voice probably wouldn't carry beyond the inside of his helmet.

But the man heard.

"I'm trying," he said. "I feel so weak . . ."

Tom supported him and helped the pilot twist on the helmet. The snap telling of a secure fit was enough for Tom to act. He opened the air flow on the man's oxygen bottle, then hoisted him up. In the zero-gravity of the ship, moving the disabled man was easy.

"Come on, just a little further," Tom encouraged over the deafening noise of the radio interference.

He hesitated in the airlock of the cargo ship. The jump over had been smooth. Going back, he'd have to take into account the added mass of the pilot. And he couldn't rely on any aid from the half-comatose man!

"Here goes nothing," he declared. He straightened his legs and aimed directly for the yawning airlock of the *Hawking*. At first, he thought nothing had happened, then noticed gradual changes in their relative position. He and the pilot moved at less than a quarter of the speed that had gotten Tom to the cargo ship. Yet, while this trip between ships took longer, Tom's aim was as good as ever.

The only thing he worried about was the added exposure to the radiation as they drifted.

"Touchdown!" Tom cried as his feet hit the metal of the science ship. The pilot's bulk was harder to stop, but Tom succeeded. With another few minutes of wrestling, he had the man inside and strapped down on the tiny bunk near the control room.

Tom stripped off the pilot's helmet and spacesuit to check for injuries. As far as he could tell from his brief but thorough examination, the only damage done to the man was from the solar flare. There weren't any broken bones and only a slight scrape marred the side of his face where he had slid against the wall.

"Thanks," the man said, blinking and peering up into Tom's blue eyes. "You saved my life!"

Chapter Two

"Maybe not," Tom said grimly. "We were outside for a long time while we were coming back. I think I can handle the radiation, but you'd already gotten a strong dosage."

The man closed his eyes and shuddered slightly.

"I knew I should have stayed on the Moon, that I should never have taken this cargo. But it was good money and I needed it."

"For what?" asked Tom gently, trying to keep the man from worrying about his troubles.

"Family. I've got a wife and two children. I've always wanted to go to the stars, be on the ship *Daniel Boone*, but the family has to eat. So I'm stuck on a cargo scow shuttling boxes from one place to another. And now I'm a dead man."

Tom was studying a panel of instruments over the bunk. Every single section of wall was studded with meters and detecting devices, since space was at a premium in this small, powerful little ship.

Suddenly his eyes lighted up. "Maybe not!" he said.

"What do you mean?" the man asked. "You're not just giving me false hope, are you?"

"Nothing like it," Tom replied. "The worst of the flare apparently passed while we were still in the *Ponderous*. When we drifted between ships, we of course accumulated some more millirads of radiation, but I don't think it's anything that can't be treated at *New America* with Gamma-null."

The man heaved a sigh of relief. Then he studied Tom closely. "Who are you?" he asked.

"I'm Tom Swift. I was out investigating a black hole moving through the Solar System."

"*The* Tom Swift?" the man asked, obviously impressed. "I'm Woody, Woody Bragg." He was quiet for a few seconds, then added, "Imagine, saved by a kid who's been to another star. You were on the *Daniel Boone*, weren't you?"

Tom almost blushed. He had expected gratitude for saving the man's life, but he hadn't counted on hero worship, especially not from a man old enough to be his father. Still, for an eighteen-year-old, Tom had gotten around. He had made numerous deep-space trips and had met with aliens from other star systems. His hyperspace-drive-powered ship, the *Exedra*, spanned light years in a fraction of a second.

He smiled at Woody Bragg. "Just take it easy and we'll hightail it back to *New America* as fast as we can. Aside from being a little on the battered side, I think you're going to make it." Tom tried to sound encouraging even though he didn't feel it. He wasn't a doctor, but he saw at a glance that the cargo pilot's condition was serious.

"Thanks," the pilot said. Tom wasn't sure whether he was thanking him for the reassurance about his condition, for rescuing him, or simply for being Tom Swift.

"What were you carrying that was so important that you'd go out during a solar flare warning?" Tom asked. If he kept the man's mind off his injuries, any pain he felt might be more bearable.

"Usual cargo. Computer chips. They're all ruined now by the radiation, I guess. Some medical supplies. Not much else. And there wasn't any flare warning."

"There wasn't?" Tom was incredulous. "That was a big·flare—there should have been a warning. Usually the solar observatory picks up the worst ones."

"No warning," the pilot repeated, his voice firm and sure. "I had a feeling this trip would turn sour, so I checked everything. The old rust bucket was in good shape—and there wasn't even a hint of flare activity before I blasted."

Tom frowned as he settled down into his contoured seat and fastened the seat buckles. His darting eyes checked all the meters and instruments. The black hole was beyond the range of his equipment now, but that didn't matter. It was more important to get back to *New America*. He took one last look at the computer readout on the solar flare. This one had definitely been over when he and Woody Bragg were in space. But there might be more.

And Tom had to admit that he hadn't received any solar storm warning either before he left. Someone had either been mighty careless, or a sun flare had taken many knowledgeable scientists by surprise!

"Help me," the pilot suddenly cried out. "I feel so . . ." His voice trailed off and ended in a low moan of pain. Anxious, Tom turned and checked the readouts showing the man's condition.

It had worsened.

"Hang on," Tom said grimly. "I'll get you back

to *New America* and the best doctors in the Solar System."

His hands worked on the controls of the *Hawking* with great assurance. He knew how to get the most speed out of it.

An alarm bell rang suddenly, startling the young inventor. Quick glances at a half dozen meters confirmed that another flare threatened to burst forth from the Sun at any moment! Tom's sensitive instruments picked up the slightest variation in the solar constant. This unusual sunspot activity on the Sun's surface produced the deadly curtains of radiation he had to avoid at all costs. Woody Bragg's condition didn't permit even the slightest added exposure now.

"If . . . if I die, tell my wife," the man said, reaching out to Tom. Even though the young inventor couldn't feel the touch through the thick fabric of his spacesuit, he knew the pilot's hand would weaken quickly.

"I've got *New America* in my navigational sights now," he said reassuringly. "A quick docking and you're home free."

Woody Bragg slumped back, his face gray with shock and strain. *New America* still lay a considerable distance off, even though Tom had picked up the giant space station's beacon.

He heaved a sigh of relief when he sighted their target. As always, a shiver of awe went down his spine when he came into view of the three-mile-long steel cylinder. It was one of mankind's greatest achievements, marking the departure of the human race from the Earth. More than 50,000 men and women lived permanently aboard *New America*, proudly calling it home. They were all pioneers, and Tom was pleased to be one of them.

"Tom Swift to *New America*," he radioed.

The burst of static over the earphones almost deafened him. The flare predicted by his instruments had already begun to chop up radio communication.

". . . to Swift, over," came the weak reply.

"Bragg's badly injured. Exposed to neutrons from the solar flare. Prepare a med team to meet us at the central docking area," Tom shouted. The fuzz and roar of static made him wonder how much had gotten through.

"Are we there yet?" Bragg asked in a wavering voice.

"Almost. Hang on. We're making the approach now," Tom assured the man. He stood the science ship on a long tongue of flame, spun around until he matched velocities perfectly, then cut off the engines.

The docking bay located at the center of the giant cylinder opened like a grinning mouth. Thick rods poked out automatically and grabbed on to either side of the ship's hull. Tom felt the *Hawking* being pulled in.

"Just in time, too," he said to himself. The instruments showing solar flare activity were creeping upward into the danger area. It wasn't safe to be outside after the LED display started flashing red!

He checked the pilot. The man's breathing had turned shallow, and he had a thready, weak pulse that Tom recognized as a symptom of shock. But the doctors on *New America* would now have the chance to save him. They were only a short distance away in the safety of the space colony.

A sudden jerking tossed Tom around the tiny cockpit like a pea in the hold of an old-time sailing ship. He forced himself back into the contoured seat and fastened the belt.

"What's going on?" he called over the radio. "I've a sick man in here. He can't take a jolting like that."

Only static greeted him. He peered out the glassite porthole at the space station. The cylinder, one mile in diameter, spun at a constant rate of one revolution every 114 seconds to give Earth-normal gravity along the rim, but at the center, where the docking bay was located, everything floated in zero-gee.

What Tom saw turned him cold inside. The

automatic equipment for the docking had jammed! Without this computer-run control, Tom was trapped. The forward hatch was blocked by a flexible metal tube that should have allowed exit from the ship. In its half-extended state, it prevented anyone from leaving.

Even worse, the *Hawking* was firmly held by the rods on either side. As long as he was locked in, he couldn't maneuver the spaceship around to another docking bay.

Ordinarily, an equipment malfunction wasn't serious. But now Tom's blue eyes glanced in anguish at the readout from his instruments. The solar flare was building in intensity. If he and Woody Bragg didn't leave the ship for the safety of *New America* within the next few minutes, they would die—and not slowly.

"Mayday!" Tom called over and over, as sweat poured down his forehead. "The equipment in the central docking bay is jammed. Someone help us!"

Chapter Three

As he spoke Tom's hands furiously worked on the controls, but the docking rods thwarted him at every turn. They were built to withstand forces far greater than he could exert with his ship's weak side-steering rockets. Turning, twisting— all the maneuvers he tried didn't work.

The LED display on the radiation counter kept reading higher and higher. Tom imagined he could feel the individual neutrons blasting through his body and leaving a trail of deadly ionization behind. That wasn't possible to feel, but he knew it was happening because of the instrument readouts.

22   No amount of work produced the slightest re-

sults. He and Woody Bragg would be fried within minutes!

"Come in, *New America*, please come in," Tom pleaded in a hoarse voice. "We're trapped in the docking bay mechanism. Someone help us."

"Certainly, Tom. It is my pleasure to be of service."

For a moment, Tom could hardly believe his ears. Aristotle, the robot he had designed and built, had heard him!

"Aristotle!" he yelled. "The docking equipment has malfunctioned. Go into the nodule and activate the manual override on the entry mechanism. And hurry. The solar flare is building!"

"I am aware of that," the mechanoid replied. "My sensorframe is very advanced, as you well know. I perceived immediately the danger to your relatively fragile human body as soon as I analyzed the data."

"Right." Tom was used to the robot's lectures. "Now just hurry."

Aristotle appeared in the control nodule. Tom heaved a sigh of relief when the automatic equipment began to work as it should. The *Hawking* slowly adjusted itself in the docking bay and the flexible tube snugly fit down over the forward hatch. Tom pressed the OPEN button and was rewarded with a flood of fresh air.

"Aristotle, quick, help me with this man," he said.

The mechanoid glided up silently, and they moved the injured pilot out the hatch, down the tube, and to the staging area outside the control nodule.

"The docking computer has been damaged by solar flare radiation," Aristotle explained. "The gentleman with you has a similar problem, I see."

"Where's the ambulance I asked for?" Tom looked about frantically for signs that the man would be taken to the hospital.

"My circuit sister is bringing one," Aristotle said proudly.

"Anita Thorwald?" In spite of the seriousness of the situation, Tom had to laugh. Anita had a biomechanoid leg which replaced her natural one crushed in an accident. When Tom had first activated Aristotle, the computer built into Anita's leg had been used to guide the robot. Since then, Aristotle and the pretty, redheaded girl had developed an unspoken system of communication that had proven valuable many times. And Anita's abilities only began with this talent.

"Tom!" She now shouted, as she guided an electricity-powered cart expertly toward the group.

"Boy, am I glad to see you!" Tom exclaimed. "We have a really sick guy on our hands. Help me load him aboard, Aristotle."

While he and Aristotle strapped the man to the bed of the cart, the fiery redhead impatiently drummed her fingers on the steering wheel.

"Got it?" she demanded. "I 'feel' what he's going through, and it isn't pleasant." Tom saw the strained expression on her face. Not only could she communicate non-verbally with Aristotle, but being an empath, she had the ability to feel others' pain and emotions.

"To the hospital. And don't spare the juice," Tom told her, as he slipped into the seat next to her.

"Always the big shot," she joked. "I didn't know you could fix speeding tickets."

Aristotle, who was standing on the cart's bumper, was almost thrown off when Anita accelerated. Anyone seeing her drive might have thought she was being reckless. But Tom knew better. Anita had the cart under perfect control all the way to the hospital.

As they pulled up, Tom saw two orderlies with a stretcher in front of the entrance. "We have an emergency case!" he called out. "Radiation from the solar flares."

"Okay," one of the men said as they approached to take Woody Bragg out of the cart.

"He'll be all right," Tom said to Anita and put his hand on her shoulder. "Don't worry."

She nodded. "Still, those solar flares should have been predicted. This shouldn't have happened," she said.

"True."

The three went into the waiting room. A nurse informed them that the doctors were treating Bragg as quickly as his condition allowed.

"At least we've got Gamma-null to counteract radiation effects," Tom said. "That's one product my dad invented that'll save lives."

"Glad to hear it," came a cheerful voice. "And here's something that'll save my ailing bank account."

Tom turned to see another friend, Ben Walking Eagle, come in.

"Take a look at this," Ben said.

Tom took the flyer the Cherokee thrust at him and shook his head. "Not another contest, Ben? You never win anything. What makes you think you'll come up with a snappy-enough name for a new soda pop?"

"It's a cinch. As soon as I get some computer time, I'll have the computer give me a printout of all possible names. And this is big! It's the first soda pop ever manufactured in space. It needs a name—and I'll win the contest."

"If anyone can program a computer to win, it's you," Tom said, laughing. His friend was a topflight programmer. If Ben said it could be done, Tom didn't doubt it for a minute.

"But do you really need a computer?" Tom asked. "I'll bet I can come up with as good a name—and without tying up valuable machine time."

Ben shook his head. "You're smart, but this calls for analytical evaluation."

Anita read the flyer. "They *do* promise a fabulous first prize," she noted. "Although they don't say what it is. But this company's not a fly-by-night outfit." Then she glanced at Ben. "I agree with Tom about not needing a computer to win. What this really needs is a woman's touch."

Ben groaned. "What have I done? I wanted to win. Now I've got two competitors."

Aristotle's violet-blue eye lenses scanned the flyer. "I see nothing limiting this contest to humans," he spoke up.

"Aristotle, why would *you* want to enter?" Ben challenged. "You don't drink soda pop. It'd rust your insides."

"Technically, my stainless steel will not rust. Tom is a much more thoughtful creator than you give him credit for, Ben."

They were interrupted by a doctor.

"You're Tom Swift? The one who brought

the cargo pilot in? I'm Doctor Lin. We used Gamma-null and he's doing fine. He'll make a complete recovery in about a week. Congratulations."

"Thanks have to go to Aristotle and Anita, too," Tom said modestly. He felt uncomfortable in the limelight. "They really saved the day."

"Congratulations to all three of you, then," the doctor said. "There're too few of us out in space to throw away even a single life."

"Good going, old pal!" Ben exclaimed, slapping his friend on the back. "And now that *that's* off your mind, how about something to eat?"

"That sounds like a wonderful idea," Tom agreed. "I haven't had anything in a space age!"

Anita laughed. "If you'll treat me, I'll drive you over to Samson's. They have great hamburgers."

"It's a deal!" Tom said, and the foursome left the hospital.

At the restaurant, they found a window booth, and the humans were soon munching on delicious charcoal-broiled hamburgers while Aristotle watched.

When they were finished, Ben pulled out a dozen pages of computer printout.

"You wanted this information," he said to Tom, "so I ran it through the machine while you were out being a hero. I'm not sure I can make head or tail of it, so let me in on the secret, will you?"

"What is it?" Anita asked.

"The data on the black hole," Tom replied. "I asked Ben to analyze it."

He took the material and skimmed through it. His brows furrowed and he bit his lip. "This isn't what I expected," he said. "My instruments were directed toward the black hole, but I picked up all the solar flare activity. This indicates the radiation levels on the Sun—" He stopped and continued reading; then he turned white.

"What's wrong, Tom?" Anita asked.

"It's hard to believe," Tom said, and his voice sounded hoarse. "But this data shows conclusively that the Sun is going to explode!"

Anita gasped. "What?"

"That's right," Tom cried. "And when the Sun goes nova, all life in the Solar System will be destroyed!"

Chapter Four

Ben and Anita stared at Tom, unable to comprehend what he had just said. Aristotle's eyes blinked slowly on and off.

"You mean . . . we'll all be killed?" Anita cried. Then she took a deep breath and settled herself. "What can we do about it?"

"I'm not sure," Tom replied grimly. "It's not something that's ever happened before. I have to make certain this data is right. To go off on a tangent without real proof won't do any good. It can only cause panic."

"Well, you've got me panicked," Ben declared. "I don't want the Sun to blow up."

"We'll have to see if we can find out what's

causing it," Tom replied. "I want to call Dad in Shopton. Maybe someone at Swift Enterprises has been looking into this."

Tom, Ben, Anita, and Aristotle left the restaurant and went quickly to the nearest communication booth. Tom punched in his ID number for billing and then placed the call from orbit to his father's personal phone. The elder Swift answered immediately.

"I've been wanting to get in touch with you, Tom," the older man said. His face was haggard and it looked as if he and sleep had been strangers for too long.

"About the Sun?" Tom asked cautiously. Much of the communication between *New America* and Earth was randomly monitored. He didn't want to alarm anyone.

"Exactly. Sunspot activity is at an all-time high. Almost two thousand millionths of the Sun's entire surface is covered with sunspots."

"Twice as much as the largest number on record!" Tom cried. "No wonder we're getting such dangerous flares."

Even as he spoke, the picture and voice from Earth began to waver and break apart. Static from the solar activity took its toll.

"Then you're sure something's wrong?" Tom shouted to make himself heard.

". . . might be nova," was all the youth heard in reply. Then his father's face turned into purple and green splotches as the comlink broke entirely.

"That's pretty bad," Ben said. "If both you and your dad agree, we're all goners."

"No!" Tom said forcefully. "We can't just roll over and play dead. We've got to start right away to study this, to work out a way of stopping it."

Aristotle spun on his base and said, "If I might interject a word of despair, Tom. When a star begins the cycle leading to ultimate explosion, no force in the universe is powerful enough to stop it. I am only a flawed mechanism, but my calculations show that the Sun is—"

"Do you want to be reprogrammed, Aristotle?" Tom asked.

Aristotle shook his mechanical head.

"Good. No more pessimism." Tom chuckled.

"What do we do first?" Anita asked. Since the first fright she had shown, she had composed herself and was ready to work against the danger confronting mankind.

"Inform Doctor Connors. He's the research director on *New America* and can aid us with information gathered from all the experiments scattered around the colony," Tom replied.

The four friends hurried in the direction of

the director's office, only to find the reception overflowing with angry citizens. Tom stiffened when he heard what one of them was saying.

"It's all Swift's fault. He shouldn't have been out there poking around that black hole. *That's* what's causing it."

"Please," Dr. Connors said in an agitated voice from the far side of the room. "Everyone leave now. Let me study the information. There'll be a public statement soon. Until then, there's no danger to anyone inside *New America*. The colony's shielding is sufficient to stop any radiation."

The crowd dispersed, muttering and shoving. Tom pressed himself against a cool metal wall to let the people out. He was glad they didn't notice him.

"You, out," came the order. "I've got a lot of work to do."

Dr. Lewis Connors was a short, bald, rotund man who had been transferred to *New America* only recently. The high forehead and rounded dome glistened with sweat, as much from the heated comments as from the room temperature.

"I want to talk to you about the Sun flares," Tom said.

Dr. Connors squinted at him, and then his face clouded over when he recognized the blond youth. "You're this Swift kid that's got them all stirred up!" he said. "Come on in." The research director glared at Tom and his entourage, and made no effort to stop Aristotle, Ben, and Anita when they followed the young inventor into the cramped inner office.

"You had no business going out and studying that black hole," Connors said without preamble. "It probably triggered this solar menace facing us."

"Impossible," Tom said firmly. "I wasn't doing anything but recording and observing."

"Who can say what the effect is on a black hole? You know that the very act of observing creates changes. That's the Heisenberg Uncertainty Principle," the man parried. "Besides, you didn't get authorization from my office."

"I didn't need it!" Tom said hotly. "Science isn't something you can regulate like a parking meter."

"May I interject a word of caution?" cut in Aristotle. "This is a serious matter. Your arguments do nothing but waste valuable time."

"You're right, Aristotle," Tom said, chagrined. "I'm sorry I blew up, Doctor Connors."

The small man settled down into a chair, but his expression didn't change.

"Here's a complete readout on Tom's experiment, Doctor Connors," Ben spoke up. He pushed the computer information across the broad metal desk toward the director.

Lewis Connors didn't even bother to glance at it.

"I don't care about this juvenile pastime. Do you realize the panic these flares are causing?"

"Of course I do." Tom's gaze squarely met the director's. "I rescued a cargo pilot. He was in bad shape from the intense radiation damage done to him during the first flare."

"At least that's one thing you did right. About the only one."

Anita had reached the end of her patience, and was ready to tell off the research director. "Look, Doctor Connors—" she began when Ben interrupted her.

"Never mind, Anita. Doctor Connors isn't interested in saving the human race. He's more interested in pinning the blame on Tom."

"Saving the human race?" snorted the director. "What drama, what absurdity!"

"My father agrees with my findings. The Sun is in danger of blowing up." Tom fought to keep his voice level and calm. It would do no one any good if he got mad now.

"Your father agrees," taunted Dr. Connors. "That's supposed to mean something, isn't it? Let me tell you, Mister Swift. Your meddling ways have caused this solar upset. I'm banning you from doing any more direct observation of that black hole."

"But Tom didn't do anything!" protested Ben.

Tom put his hand on his friend's shoulder. The Indian quieted down and grabbed the computer data off the director's desk. Without another word, he angrily left the office. Anita stomped out after him.

"Why do you think I'm responsible?" asked Tom.

"The black hole has changed course," Connors replied. "Not much, but enough. Only you could have caused it. Now get out of my sight before I call Security and have you thrown out."

The man bent over his desk and started to read a report flashing on his computer screen. Tom and Aristotle followed their friends out to the street.

The young inventor hadn't taken two steps when he noticed the crowd that had been in the director's outer office had not dispersed. They had remained clustered near the door. And they were ominously quiet. He felt every single person staring at him. Finally one man stepped forward.

"You're the one who caused the flares. You're Tom Swift!"

"I'm Tom Swift," the youth admitted, "but I had nothing to do with the flares."

"He's lying," someone in the back shouted. "Let's get him!"

The people grew noisy and surged forward. Tom saw that reasoning with them was impossible. He hated to back down when he was right, but these colonists were angry and afraid. They'd take out their frustration on anyone they caught. Tom happened to be handy.

"Tom, here!" Anita cried. He turned and saw her in the electric cart. She and Ben had slipped away when they saw the lingering mob and prepared for a quick escape.

Tom jumped in. As threats were shouted by the crowd, the three humans raced off.

"Aristotle!" cried Tom. "He's still back there. We have to rescue him."

"He got away," Anita said. "Don't worry about him. Now, where do you want to go?"

"Straight to my lab," Tom replied. "We have a lot of work to do. And I don't have the slightest idea where to begin!"

Chapter Five

Anita dropped the two boys off at the lab, then left to finish a job she had been asigned while Tom had been in outer space.

"It won't take more than a few hours to wind it all up," she said. "See you then."

"Right," Tom said. "And hurry. We need all the help we can get."

He and Ben had been working for about forty-five minutes when Aristotle walked in.

"Where've you been, tin man?" Ben asked. "Anita said you took off when you saw the mob in front of Doctor Connors's office. Weren't in the mood to fight, were you?"

"Fighting would have accomplished nothing,"

the robot said in his logical fashion. "I left to inform the police in case you got into trouble. But then I saw Anita arriving with the cart."

"Took you a long time to get here," Tom grumbled.

"I went to talk with the main computer to see if I could pick up any information on the solar flares," Aristotle told him. "But things are so busy over there that I did not have a chance."

Tom grinned. "Thanks for trying, Aristotle."

The robot nodded his head. "I presume you have analyzed all the available data by now," he said. "What is your opinion?"

Ben stared at a sheet of paper in front of him. "The star Elira will blow up in less than a week," he said.

Aristotle did not comment. Instead, he looked at Tom. The young inventor leaned back in his chair and locked his strong fingers behind his head. He stared out the end of his observatory, past the equipment littering the lab, into the vastness of space. Millions of diamond-hard points stared back at him, each a star, each with its own special secrets waiting to be discovered.

"That's a curious coincidence," Tom said. "Our Sun is beginning to show instability, and this other star is on the brink of going nova, too. Elira's only about fifteen light years away?"

"Right," Ben answered. He tapped the stack of computer readouts in front of him. "There's no question it'll explode soon. The odds are astronomical against two stars this close together going nova at the same time.

Tom winced at his friend's pun. He bent over his computer console and punched in a few numbers, then said, "This proves my investigation of the black hole had nothing to do with the Sun's flares. Elira is in the opposite direction from the black hole's orbit through space."

"The odds," Aristotle declared, "are definitely in favor of another cause for the flares. But what might it be, Tom? I am not programmed to make such an evaluation."

"Whatever I said, Aristotle, would be a guess, and not backed up with facts," Tom replied. "We need hard evidence to give to Doctor Connors. The solar flares are getting worse. Even *New America*'s shielding won't keep out the radiation if they increase much more. As it is, all comlinks with Earth, except for the line-of-sight lasercoms, are out."

"Have you talked with your dad about this?" Aristotle asked.

"No. The lines are jammed too much for me to get through. Everyone's anxious to let their friends and families on Earth know they're doing all right."

Tom turned back to the tedious but necessary work at hand. He took spectral readings of all nearby stars and kept a close watch on the Sun. Hours passed. He was very tired, but still he and Ben kept working.

Finally, Ben spoke up. "What idiots we've been! The answer's right in front of us. It's been there all the time."

"What's that?" Tom asked, his mind less than sharp.

"We just load everyone into spaceships with stardrives and go somewhere else. I'm sure the Skree would take us in. Commander Mok N'Ghai owes us a lot for what we did." Ben was referring to the insectoid race they'd met in *The War in Outer Space*. Mok N'Ghai had become a good friend during the battle.

"I am sorry, Ben," Aristotle stated, "but your plan is not feasible. If you were not so sleepy, I am sure you would see why."

Ben blinked, then rubbed his eyes. Sleep did fuzz his brain, but he didn't understand what the mechanoid meant.

"What Aristotle's saying," Tom explained, "is that there aren't enough ships equipped with the faster-than-light drive. Only our *Exedra* is ready to go, in any case. This kind of a migration involving billions of people would take generations. We have only months. Perhaps only weeks."

Ben sighed. "You're right, Tom. And so are you, rust bucket. I hate it when you're right."

"Why?" Aristotle asked. "I am programmed to respond correctly to both mathematical and logical problems."

"Never mind. I'm so tired I'd do better spending my time thinking up names for the soda pop."

"You're still working on that?" Tom asked in amazement. "In spite of all this?"

"It gives me a break for a few minutes. Sort of lets me know what we're trying to save everyone for."

They turned back to work until Ben finally declared, "This is it. The Swift Enterprises minicomputer is a dandy, but it's too small for the kind of stuff I'm putting in. Do you think Doctor Connors will let us near the main computer after that crowd almost lynched you?"

Tom shrugged. "With this information about Elira I can prove I wasn't responsible. Doctor Connors is a scientist. He'll listen to reason."

Neither Ben nor Aristotle seemed convinced.

"I have all the data I can carry," Tom went on. "But the new spectroscopic readings need to be taken in another half hour." He was torn between going to Dr. Connors and remaining.

"I will be happy to stay here and perform this function, Tom," Aristotle spoke up. "I have no desire to see your youthful enthusiasm crushed when Doctor Connors refuses to listen."

Ben and Tom exchanged glances, then smiled. Aristotle sometimes lacked real knowledge of human behavior. Dr. Connors *had* to listen to them. They had hard facts to show him.

"Go on, Aristotle. We'll be back in an hour or so."

"Good-bye, Tom. Stay away from large gatherings of hostile colonists."

Tom didn't need the warning. He and Ben made their way to the research director's office through back corridors.

"He's busy," an assistant in the outer office told them. "He won't be able to see anyone for the next couple of days."

"But we must talk to him," Ben insisted. "Our computer analysis has turned up another star about ready to explode. It's in the other direction from where the black hole orbited. That means—"

"I don't care what it means!" the man cut in. "Things are pretty hot around here, and I have strict orders not to let anyone in, especially Tom Swift. Now please leave!"

"You don't understand. He and I are working on the same problem and I came up with some new data that he would *want* to see!"

"If you don't leave instantly, I'm calling the guards," the assistant said curtly.

Ben shook his head, then brushed a strand of black hair out of his eyes. "Come on, Tom. We're wasting our time."

Tom nodded, too angry to speak. When they were outside, he took a deep breath. "We have to go on despite him. This is too important to simply drop at the first sign of opposition."

"Now you're talking!" Ben regained his normal good humor. "They laughed at Tesla when he invented alternating-current motors. The people thought the world was flat. They've been wrong, while a very few were right. People like you, Tom."

"Come on," said Tom, smiling. "We can get in another two hours' work before catching a catnap."

They walked toward the lab, disheartened at not being able to see the research director. On the way they met Anita, who was now free to work with them.

She gritted her teeth when she heard what had happened. "It figures," she fumed.

"I don't see any reason why I can't tap into the main computer," Ben said, his voice low and conspiratorial. "They can't catch me. I know all the entry codes."

"That's why I hang around with a technical genius," Tom said. "Not only can you make it jump through hoops, you've learned to spy on it whenever it isn't kowtowing to you."

"Me, a genius?" the Cherokee scoffed. "I'm only a computer jockey." He opened the door to the laboratory, then stood stock-still and cried out in horror. "Oh, no!"

"What's wrong?" Tom pushed past his friend and gasped. "I don't believe this! Someone wrecked all our equipment!"

Ben clenched his teeth, then muttered, "This will put us back days. And some of the stuff can't be replaced without ordering spare parts from Earth."

Tom went into the lab and felt broken glass grinding under the soles of his shoes. Then he spied something that made him feel sick to his stomach.

"Aristotle!" he screamed. "They wrecked Aristotle, too! They killed him!"

Chapter Six

The mechanoid lay partially dismembered, pieces scattered all over the room. Only a tiny glow in the left eye lens revealed any life at all.

"He'll never be the same, Tom," Anita wailed. "There's too much damage!"

Tom was already surveying the situation in detail. "It's not as bad as it looks," he finally said. "I can rebuild him."

"You can?" she asked, doubt in her voice.

"Sure. You and Ben give me a hand."

The three started to work, first cleaning up the lab and then sorting out the undamaged parts. Tom's efforts took on a feverish quality until he began to see results. Finally, Aristotle stood before them, only a few scratches on his stainless-steel frame.

"He's whole," Ben said, "in body. But his programming is gone. What made him Aristotle is lost."

Tom smiled broadly and shook his head. "Give me a little more credit than that." He opened a small box that hadn't been touched by their intruders. Inside lay a gleaming silver cylinder.

"A duplicate of Aristotle's memory!" Anita exclaimed.

"Not an exact one since I made this a few weeks ago, but it'll be close. Aristotle might not remember anything about the attack, though."

"You mean he'll have amnesia?" Ben chuckled.

"Maybe. But there was some life left in him when we first found him. A small current might hold memories. We'll have to activate him and see."

Tom inserted the cylinder into a slot in Aristotle's left shoulder. For a moment nothing happened; then the mechanoid's eyes began to glow. They flashed and finally he spoke.

"Tom, it is good to see you again."

"You remember what happened?" Tom asked anxiously.

"Vaguely. It is as if a curtain has been pulled across, yet I see dim outlines. It is very confusing.

I am unable to access those memories with any certainty."

"I can help," said Anita. "Let's link my leg computer with Aristotle. We might be able to clear up some of that fog."

Tom and Ben exchanged glances. "It's worth a try," the young inventor said.

Anita quickly plugged a cable into the computer controlling her right leg. Aristotle took the other end of the cable and inserted it in the appropriate place on his left side.

Tom and Ben watched in fascination as Anita began slowly tapping the computer controls installed in the wristwatchlike device on her right arm. She gave them the high sign and smiled when a tiny green light flashed on the control.

"Three men entered the room under false pretenses," Aristotle said in his old, positive voice. "I see it all quite clearly, thanks to Anita's unscrambling that portion of my memory."

Anita smiled broadly, glad to have been able to restore her friend to full working ability.

"They claimed to have a delivery of important parts for you," Aristotle continued. "I allowed them in. One struck me with a wrench. You should not leave such things lying about, Ben. It is dangerous."

Ben scowled but said nothing. Tom had been

hounding him about leaving tools around, too.

"I know, I know," he said. "Sorry, Aristotle. I wasn't counting on a break-in."

"Go on, Aristotle," Tom urged. "Describe the men."

"I have never seen them before. However, I did recognize their jumpsuits. More precisely, I recognized the insignia on their sleeves, a white circle pierced by a sword on a starfield."

"The Luna Corporation emblem!" Tom exclaimed.

"I thought when Luna was captured on the planet Aquilla, it would be the end of him!" Ben muttered, referring to their adventure in *Ark Two*.

"He may be back, and he *is* your enemy," Aristotle pointed out. He did not need to mention all the dirty tricks the competitive and dishonest industrialist had played on Tom Swift since they first met in *The Alien Probe*.

"I don't understand," Tom said, perching on the edge of a desk. "If I'm right about the solar flares being the start of the Sun going nova, Luna and his men have nothing to gain by stopping me from investigating the matter. And if I'm wrong, why bother at all?"

"One of them mentioned Elira," the mechanoid said slowly. His eyes flashed. "Yes, it is all coming back to me now. Their leader mentioned a Luna Corporation project on Elira."

"Elira!" Anita exclaimed. "That's the star that's going to blow up! I wonder if they're aware—"

"Tom, incoming message," Ben interrupted her. "It's from your father."

"Good," Tom said. "I need to ask him some questions. I just hope he can help." He went to the comlink at the end of the laboratory nodule and flipped the switch to ACCEPT. The elder Swift's worried face filled the screen.

"Tom, I'm glad I finally got through. Communication has been almost impossible." But even as he spoke, the picture began to jumble, and his words were gradually drowned out by static.

"Dad, let me ask you—"

Tom was cut off by the elder Swift. "No time. This is vital. Swift Enterprises scientists have picked up signs that a new and devastating solar flare is on the way. I tried to contact Doctor Connors, but he wasn't available. Tell him that he must take every precaution. This is. . ." The rest of the words were lost in a roar of static. The picture broke up, and the comlink was lost in solar radiation.

"A new flare," Ben said, shaking his head. "If your father is this worried, it must be a whopper."

Tom spun dials and fine-tuned the radio, to no avail. "I can't even reach the control center," he said in exasperation.

"Try the communications laser," Anita suggested. "That's on a light beam and won't be scrambled up."

"It'll take me a while. It got knocked out of alignment."

The young inventor knitted his brows for a moment, then said, "We'll have to split up so we don't waste any time. Anita, you and Ben go to Doctor Connors's office. Meanwhile, Aristotle and I will work on the lasercom and try to reach someone in authority."

Anita nodded. "At least one of us ought to get through."

"I'll bet you a bottle of that new soda pop that Anita and I'll be first!" Ben said and raced to the door.

Tom chuckled. "We'll see."

Anita followed Ben, and they rushed off. Tom and Aristotle turned their attention to repairing the lasercom and tuning it properly to contact Administration, located at the far end of the cylindrical space colony.

"This break-in was very unfortunate," Aristotle said. "And it came at a terrible time."

"It could have been worse," Tom said, wiping

sweat from his forehead. "Those vandals could have smashed the ruby crystal inside the laser. If they had, we wouldn't have a chance of warning anyone before the flare hits."

"You are correct," the mechanoid answered. "It will require less than two minutes for the lasercom to warm. Another minute to locate the receptor and—Tom! We are moving!"

Tom didn't need the robot's warning to realize something was very, very wrong. Normally, inside *New America* there was no sensation of movement. The spinning space colony produced an artificial gravity that was indistinguishable from that on Earth. Now he felt the steel floor shiver and rumble.

"The flare!" he cried.

"No," Aristotle said. "The instruments do not record that danger. However, the warning lights show that the laboratory nodule has been cut off from *New America* and we are drifting into space!"

Tom rushed to a glassite window and peered out. *New America* hung in space like a long steel rod, with both ends visible. In the place where the laboratory nodule had been attached was a gaping hole.

"At least the automatic airlocks worked," Tom muttered. He had insisted these be installed in case anything happened inside his lab requiring isolation from the rest of the space colony. He was now glad he had put them in. The self-closing doors had saved his life. Without them, all the air in the lab would have rushed into the vacuum of space.

"This is another act of sabotage on David Luna's part," he went on angrily. "Why is he doing this? He's endangering everyone aboard the space station."

Aristotle spun on his motorframe and faced Tom. "We are drifting away from *New America* at approximately forty feet per second."

"I have to tell them about the flare," Tom said, hurrying his preparations. As the lasercom warmed up, he aimed it toward a receiving antenna at the far end of the colony.

"Administration," a soft voice announced.

Tom passed along his father's warning concerning the new solar flare. Then he told the woman at the other end of his plight.

"Sorry, Mister Swift," she apologized. "There's no way we can send a rescue party for you. Not now, not with all the preparations we need to make to weather this radiation storm."

"I understand," Tom said. But an ice cold hand seemed to grip his heart.

"I'm . . . sorry," the woman repeated, with real sympathy in her voice.

Tom didn't blame her at all. In space the

slightest hesitation meant death. There wasn't time to organize a rescue party. Even if there had been time, a space tug coming out to pull the lab nodule back would be exposed to the full violence of the flare.

And Tom didn't want others dying in a futile attempt to save him.

"Tom," Aristotle said softly. "The radiation level from the solar flare is rising. Your father was right in stating that this one is the worst yet."

Red lights flashed ominously in every direction Tom looked!

Chapter Seven

"The radiation shielding in the central portion of the nodule is adequate for you to survive," the mechanoid went on. "My calculations show that the lead shielding used for experimentation will provide ample protection."

"Will you be all right?" Tom asked anxiously.

"My memory components are well shielded," the robot replied. "There is little else in my sensorframe or motorframe requiring such protection."

"Good."

"There is one further point of concern," the robot said. "Humans require oxygen. Since this nodule is no longer attached to the main air supply furnished by the space colony, you will require additional oxygen soon."

"This is a big laboratory, Aristotle," Tom pointed out. "If I lie down and breathe slowly, I can make it last."

"Perhaps," the mechanoid said. "But it will be close. If the radiation storm takes no longer than half an hour, there will be no problem. However—"

"Let's not think beyond that," Tom cut his robot short. He crouched behind the thick lead shielding and tried to relax. But instead he imagined the deadly particles missing him by inches. The radiation counters clicked madly. Minutes stretched into a half hour.

Tom was fighting panic. The air began to taste stale. It hurt his lungs to breathe. He looked at Aristotle, waiting for some signal of reassurance, a word of comfort. But the robot stood motionless.

Still, the solar flare's intensity did not slacken. Tom felt lightheaded. Controlling his breathing became harder and harder. He panted heavily, trying to force enough oxygen into his lungs.

But there wasn't enough in the air!

Stop! Please stop! Tom moved his lips but was unable to make a sound. The deadly radiation continued to fill the lab all around him.

Finally Tom lost consciousness.

Suddenly he heard a distant voice calling to him. At first he thought he only dreamed it, but then he recognized Aristotle. Struggling to breathe and focus his eyes at the same time, the young inventor looked up. The robot stood over him.

"The flare is slackening. The danger is over."

"Danger over," Tom muttered. He felt as if someone had wrapped him in a cotton blanket. Even his mouth and nostrils seemed to be filled with cotton. All he wanted to do was sleep.

That thought brought him around. If he gave in to his body's demands, he would die.

"Aristotle!" he called. "Get me the spacesuit from the emergency locker. My oxygen. No air. Need the spacesuit."

"I am sorry," the mechanoid said. "The Luna Corporation vandals destroyed its spaceworthiness. They slashed it badly."

"Did they . . . damage . . . the oxygen bottles?" Tom asked.

"No. I shall get them for you."

Aristotle returned with the damaged spacesuit. Even in his oxygen-starved daze, Tom saw that his friend had been right. The oxygen bottles were intact. He opened a nozzle near his face and inhaled deeply. The air had a metallic tang to it, but it was the sweetest-smelling perfume Tom had ever breathed.

He sat up as soon as his head cleared, wondering what to do next. He knew better than to use the lasercom to call *New America* for aid. The solar storm would have damaged much in the colony. All efforts would be turned to fixing vital systems and aiding those people who had been exposed to deadly ionizing radiation.

"I have placed a call to Ben and Anita," Aristotle told him. "They are concerned for your welfare."

"Can they get a tug out to rescue us?" Even as he asked, Tom knew the answer.

"Doctor Connors requires all spacecraft for emergency repair work. Everything must be fixed before another solar flare builds."

"And we have no rocket of our own to propel us back," Tom said glumly.

Suddenly he had an idea. "But we do!" he cried out. "This entire lab is filled with gas. What more do we need?"

He rose eagerly, motioning to his robot. "Come on, help me!"

"May I remind you of the damaged condition of the spacesuit?" Aristotle objected. "To evacuate all atmosphere, even if it is lacking oxygen, would cause your body to explode. In the vacuum of space, your blood would boil."

"Eventually. But not right away. I know it's dangerous, but it's my only hope."

"This is foolhardy, Tom."

"Do you have a better idea?"

The robot shook his head.

Tom began mending the slashed spacesuit the best he could with a special silicon rubber compound he kept in the lab. When he came to the severed leg, he sighed. The seal between portions of the suit simply wouldn't hold pressure for long.

"The best I can do is this, Aristotle," he told the mechanoid. "I'm putting the rubber sealant on my skin as well as the suit. It won't hold forever, but it ought to hold long enough. Only a small portion of my leg will be exposed to space. If I wrap it tightly enough with a bandage, that should keep the blood vessels from breaking."

"It is dangerous," Aristotle repeated. "Your chance for survival is small."

"It's better than what I've got now."

Tom added one last layer of the heavy silicon rubber sealant to the leg, then checked the instruments. He found *New America* and aimed the laser in the opposite direction, switching the power to maximum. The ruby beam lashed out, cutting cleanly through the glassite window.

Tom and Aristotle were battered around by the sudden rush of air out the hole. The blond inventor had turned the entire lab nodule into a rocket.

"It worked, Tom," Aristotle congratulated him. "We are heading toward *New America* again. However, it is not an exact course."

"It was the best I could do. By how much will we miss the colony?"

"Almost one mile."

"Tell them to have an airlock open and waiting for us. It's a long jump but I can make it." He rubbed his gloved hands over the seam along the spacesuit leg. A mile jump in the space meant exposing this faulty joint for as long as ten minutes.

While the lab nodule slowly swung back toward *New America*, Tom monitored air leakage through his damaged suit. It was minor, but increasing.

"We'll make it, Aristotle," he told the mechanoid. "As long as we don't miss."

"Someone is signalling from airlock # 23. We are nearing the point of departure," Aristotle said. Then he sighed. "I shall be sorry to lose this laboratory."

"So will I," Tom agreed, "but trading ourselves for it seems like a good deal. Ready, Aristotle? You go first."

"Yes, Tom."

The mechanoid opened the door to the vastness of space. Less than a mile away was the safety offered by *New America*.

"I shall wait for you in the airlock," he said and shot forward, his course exactly computed and perfectly aligned. Tom checked his suit pressure and found it dropping. But he had enough oxygen left, in spite of the big leak, to reach the colony.

He jumped, following Aristotle's gleaming silver form.

Cold crept up his leg where the rubber joint allowed air to seep out. Tom kept the leg stiff to avoid flexing open his makeshift patch. Closer and closer he came to the space colony. A man was standing in the airlock, waiting for him. He held up a rocket gun with a weighted line in it.

"Don't shoot it!" Tom called out. But his suit radio didn't work. He waved to the man to indicate he didn't want the safety line. But the man, in his eagerness to help, misinterpreted the gesture. He fired the emergency line.

Tom held his breath. He saw the weighted line coming directly toward him. Unless he could grasp it, it would hit him! He twisted, trying to get out of the missile's way. But to no avail! The lead weight struck him squarely in the middle of the chest before he could grab it and sent him spinning sideways!

The man had meant to help. Instead, he had altered Tom's course so that he would miss the airlock entirely. Even worse, the patch on the spacesuit leg began to gush out precious air. Tom spun off into space again, this time in a dangerously leaking suit.

He would be dead within minutes!

Chapter Eight

Tom spun out of control. Tumbling over and over, he rapidly lost all orientation. Occasionally he saw the silver flash of *New America* swing by, but he had no way of directing his motion. And all the while the repaired leg of the spacesuit leaked more and more air.

The young inventor had had enough oxygen to reach the space colony, but now he had only minutes of life left!

Suddenly, another silver flash crossed his field of vision. For a moment, Tom thought he only imagined it. Then he got a better look.

"Aristotle!" he cried, his voice echoing in the spacesuit helmet.

When the robot reached him, he wrapped the youth in strong metallic arms. The tumbling slowed due to Aristotle's stabilizing mass. Tom peered back at the space colony. The impact of the emergency line hadn't sent him sailing out into space at a very fast clip. Yet, how would they be able to return?

Then he saw what Aristotle carried. Wrapped around the mechanoid's sensorframe was another safety line. If they could be pulled back fast enough—

A sudden jerk marked the end of the line. Aristotle's powerful arms not only held Tom securely, they pressed the edges of the spacesuit leg together to slow air loss. Gradually tension on the emergency line increased, and they started back toward *New America*.

Soon they were safely inside the airlock.

"I'm sorry," the oriental man at the gate blurted. "I saw you and thought you wanted the line and I shot and . . ."

"Everything's fine," Tom said in a weary voice. "You did what you thought was right."

"If that robot of yours hadn't taken off when it did, you'd be a goner."

"Aristotle's not an 'it,'" Tom pointed out.

"No, I guess not," the man said, eyeing Aristotle. "It took a lot of courage to rescue you like he did."

"Your praise," Aristotle said, "is appreciated. Thank you, sir."

Tom examined the leg joint on the spacesuit. The brief exposure hadn't injured him at all. The tight wrapping he'd applied before putting on the suit had worked.

He turned to his mechanoid and smiled. "We made it, tin man, we made it. Thanks."

"Tom!" came a voice from down the corridor.

Tom turned to see Ben Walking Eagle running toward him.

"I'm glad you're safe," Ben cried. "Anita and I did all we could to get a rescue party together, but only Lee Yu here could be spared from his post." Ben looked at the man standing to one side.

"I wasn't much help," Lee Yu said. "Aristotle did it all." He pointed to the robot, then left, still uncomfortable about his mistake.

"He doesn't look too happy," Ben observed. "And you won't be too happy either when you hear what happened."

"The colony's been damaged? Someone's been killed by the solar flare?"

"The damage was slight enough and only a few

cases of radiation poisoning occurred. A good dose of Gamma-null will take care of them. No, Tom, it's bad news for you personally."

The young inventor steeled himself for what his friend had to say.

"Anita found a guy who works for the Luna Corporation. He told her about the break-in and how they jettisoned the lab nodule. But he's afraid of David Luna and won't make any statements openly."

"So we can't prove anything to Doctor Connors!" Tom said glumly.

"What's worse, Luna Corporation executives on *New America* have been bending Doctor Connors's ear. They've offered immense amounts of aid, both money and personnel, from their mining base on the Moon. And he's listening to them."

"Let's go talk to Doctor Connors," Tom decided. "Maybe we can persuade him he's allying himself with a pack of wolves."

"It'll have to be the best pitch you ever made," Ben muttered. "I don't think you have much chance with the research director."

"We'll have to try," Tom said.

They quickly walked to Doctor Connors's office. Anita Thorwald was storming out when they arrived. The expression on her face was a combi-

67

nation of fiery rage and confusion.

"What's wrong?" Tom asked.

"Everything. I got even more information about what David Luna has been up to. He's running experiments on a research station orbiting around Elira. Some of his own staff suspect that they have something to do with the instability of that planet and the solar flares."

"What are those people doing about it?"

"They can't do anything. You know Luna runs a tight ship and doesn't tolerate dissension. I couldn't even find out who they are. And the guy who told me won't tell Doctor Connors. As a matter of fact, he seems to have vanished into thin air."

"Did you try to see Connors?"

"He won't let me in. Tom, what are we going to do?"

"I don't know. I can't accuse Luna without proof, but if his people have done something to disturb the Sun's thermonuclear cycle, they might be trying to cover it up by blaming the solar flares on me."

"This time Doctor Connors *has* to listen to us! He can't be too busy forever," Ben stormed. He shoved through the doors and went unannounced into the inner office. Tom and Anita followed. Only Aristotle remained outside.

"What's the meaning of this?" the research director demanded. "You can't barge in here like this!"

Tom glanced across the desk at a computer console. Lights were flashing red, green, and amber, all requesting the man's time and attention. The solar flares hadn't badly damaged *New America*, but putting things back to normal took a lot of coordination of personnel and equipment. All the lines of power led to Dr. Connors's computer—and his judgment.

"We have proof that Luna Corporation is responsible for destroying Tom's lab, then chucking him and Aristotle out into space to die," Anita began.

"Proof?" the director said. "Show it to me!" His eyes kept drifting to the lights winking on and off across his console, begging for action.

"I talked to one of Luna Corporation's employees and he said that he heard that—"

"Hold it!" Dr. Connors said, raising his hand. "Young lady, that's hearsay. How do I know some disgruntled employee isn't out to get back at his superiors? Bring me the person making the charges and we'll talk directly."

"He won't come forward. He's afraid of what David Luna might do to him!"

"Then you're wasting my time again." Dr.

Connors sighed and shifted in his chair. He tented his fingers under his chin as he stared at the trio. "I've spoken with the colony board of directors. They agree with me."

Tom felt the tension mount. "Doctor Connors, don't do anything rash."

"This isn't rash, young man. My data—and that supplied by Luna Corporation research stations—continues to strongly indicate that you triggered the solar flares by your investigation of the black hole. Those flares endanger all our lives, disrupt necessary communication, and in general play havoc with life in *New America*. The board has agreed that you are to return to Earth at the earliest possible time."

"Doctor Connors," Tom pleaded, "the Luna Corporation might be responsible for the flares! They have a research station in the Elira star system. Elira is about to go nova. That's too much of a coincidence to overlook."

"Luna has research stations in many places. Tom, I've given you more time than I should have. In the past you and your father have made valuable contributions. But now my time and patience are limited. I have ordered Security to accompany you to the cargo ship lifting for Earth in one hour."

"But Doctor Connors—" Ben began.

"It's all right," Tom soothed his friend. "He's only doing what he thinks is right."

Most of the lights on the control console flashed a baleful red now. Decisions had to be made quickly. Lewis Connors turned back to them, the problem of Tom Swift solved and put out of his mind.

Tom, Ben, and Anita left the director's office and joined Aristotle outside.

"You can't let him push you around like that!" Anita blazed angrily. "You're right. He's wrong. It's that simple!"

Tom nodded, with a far-off look in his eyes. "Ben, what condition is the *Exedra* in?"

"Your starship? Well, I had just finished checking it out for a quick jaunt to see our friend Mok N'Ghai again, after you finished with the black hole."

"Then it's ready?"

"Sure."

Aristotle had moved up to the trio. "You are not thinking of disobeying the director, are you?" he queried.

Tom turned to the mechanoid. "You were eavesdropping, weren't you?"

"My auditory sensors are more acute than human ears. It is difficult for me not to pick up loud voices."

"Doctor Connors said he wanted me off *New America*. He said Earth, but he probably won't care if we go elsewhere," Tom said.

"You should tell your dad," Anita pointed out.

"Communication is still unreliable and what comlinks do work are filled with official transmissions," the mechanoid pointed out.

"Then let's get to the *Exedra* and pay Luna Corporation a visit."

"And we'd better hurry," Ben said. "Look!"

Tom turned and saw a *New America* security squad trotting down the street toward them. When their leader spotted the group, he shouted, "There they are! Get 'em!"

Tom and his friends spun around and ran, the security force hot on their heels!

Chapter Nine

Anita looked over her shoulder. The security squad was narrowing the distance between them!

"They're catching up!" she gasped.

"We only have to go a bit further," Tom urged. "We're here. Ben, get in and warm up the engines. We want a fast takeoff, but one that won't damage *New America*."

"Right." The computer expert disappeared through the hatch of the *Exedra*.

"Aristotle, do you still have the welding attachment fixed to your motorframe?" Tom asked.

"Yes. Do you want me to ready it for use?"

"Yes. Weld the airlock door shut as soon as we get inside."

Anita and Tom rushed through the space colony airlock, then slammed the heavy metal door. As soon as the young inventor had turned the wheel to ensure an airtight seal between station and door, the mechanoid applied the brilliant blue flame to the portions of the airlock that would be hardest to break through.

"Whew, just in time," Anita breathed. They heard the security force pounding on the other side of the thick steel panel.

"My spot welds will not hold them back long," Aristotle warned. "We had better make a hasty departure."

"That's exactly what I intend to do," Tom declared.

Once inside the *Exedra*, he slammed the ship's airlock and hurried to the bridge. Ben had the control computers humming and the engines hot in no time.

"Ready to blast, Tom," he called out.

"Good. Let's go!"

The engines ignited and the *Exedra* moved away from *New America*.

"Wow!" Anita breathed. "We made that just in time."

"No problem," Ben grinned. "Those guys needed a few minutes to blast through Aristotle's welding job."

"I'm not sure I want to face Doctor Connors

when we come back," Anita giggled.

"He'll send us into exile for disobeying his orders," Tom said. "But let's not worry about that now." He turned his attention to the instruments.

When the ship was far enough from the colony so that the rocket wash wouldn't damage anything, he increased power. The acceleration pushed him down into his comfortable, contoured couch.

"Lock in for Elira," he finally said to Ben.

"We've got triangulation on Canopus, Elira, and the Sun," Ben reported. "Everyone ready for the hyperspace jump?"

"I'll never really be ready for that," Anita grumbled.

"You'd better be," Ben advised. "I'm starting the countdown."

Tom, Ben, and Anita checked the buckles on their seat belts, while Aristotle braced himself against the wall.

"Three, two, one, zero!" Ben counted, and Anita took one last, deep breath.

A moment later everything reversed around them. Gravitational forces that attracted now repelled. The young people felt dizzy as the *Exedra* hurled though space at many times the speed of light. Tom tried to control his nausea and keep from passing out.

In complex ways, the force field surrounding

the ship opened a hole in space. The *Exedra* slipped into that hole and experienced time and space reversal. Near its destination, the ship came back into normal space.

"I'll never get used to it," Anita vowed. "It makes me feel as if someone's turning me inside out."

"It's not that bad," Ben told her. "In fact, it's better than drinking that soda pop we're supposed to be naming."

"You've tried it?" Tom asked. While he spoke, he made sure that everything had gone right. The stardrive was still a new technology and prone to tiny errors. He found that it had functioned perfectly.

"Yeah," Ben said, making a face. "It tastes like it's permanently turned inside out. Still, winning first prize in the contest is reason enough to enter."

"What if first prize is a year's supply?" Tom teased.

"I can use it to scrub the *Exedra*'s decks." Ben chuckled.

"Such use would not be good for the paint," Aristotle said seriously. "Most soda pops contain carbonic acid. Also, there are dyes in it that—"

"Enough!" Ben cried while Tom and Anita laughed.

"There is the Luna Corporation's space station," Tom said, shifting the radar unit slightly for a better image. "It's way in close to the star, almost in the photosphere."

"That is a very dangerous location," Aristotle said. "The star's atmosphere of gases is extremely hot."

Tom nodded. "Try to hail the station, Anita," he said. "I'll use the rocket drive to get us in closer."

The redhead worked on the comlink until she produced a signal almost drowned out by static.

"This is the best I can do," she said. "The radiation coming from Elira is producing the same sort of interference we were getting from the Sun."

"I'll run the signal through the computer and try to filter out the noise," Ben offered.

He fiddled with the controls and finally nodded for Tom to go ahead.

"This is Tom Swift aboard the *Exedra* calling Luna Corporation's research station," Tom said.

"Come in, *Exedra*," rang out the immediate response. "What are you doing here?"

"Just visiting. Request permission to dock so we can check our equipment."

"Is it an emergency?"

"No emergency, but without proper maintenance, we might have problems."

No reply came for several minutes. Tom

leaned back and waited. What he'd told them wasn't a lie. Without proper checking of the ship, problems might develop.

"Very well," came the reluctant reply.

"But don't expect any replacement parts from our storeroom. We don't have much to spare."

"Thanks," Tom said. "We can handle any repairs on our own. We have a complete machine shop aboard ship."

"Your signal is fading, *Exedra*," came a weak response. "We want to send a message rocket out and avoid further radio contact."

"A message rocket? What do they mean, Tom?" Anita demanded. "I've never heard of such a thing!"

"I never have, either."

"They've launched something, that's for sure," Ben spoke up. "It's small and coming in fast. I don't know how they could have gotten a message into a nosecone so soon."

"It is coming in *too* fast," Aristotle said in a perturbed voice. "It cannot slow down enough to match speed with us. I do not think it is a message rocket!"

Tom glanced at the radar screen, then spun in his chair and began stabbing at button after button on the control panel. The *Exedra* bucked, rockets flared, and the sudden acceleration threw them all to the side of the cabin.

"Watch it, will you?" Ben complained. "Give me some warning if you're going joy-riding."

"That was not joy-riding, as you call it," Aristotle spoke up. "Look at the screen, Ben."

In silence, they watched the rocket race past and continue on. Less than a hundred miles away, it exploded. They heard the fragments rattle on the ship's thick hull.

"They tried to blow us out of space!" Anita raged. "Why, those low-down, space-brained, thieving—"

"Getting mad will not alter their ruthlessness," Aristotle said in a calm voice. "Tom acted correctly to save us."

The blond youth reached over and flipped on the radio. The static greeting him made communication difficult, but not impossible.

"What's the meaning of the rocket attack?" Tom demanded. "We did nothing to provoke you."

"Attack?" came the crackling answer. "That wasn't an attack. The message rocket went haywire. Must be the solar flares that caused it to go off course like that."

"No solar flare caused the rocket to blow up less than a hundred miles away," Ben muttered. "If that thing had hit us, we'd be breathing space now. And they know it!"

Tom motioned to Ben for silence, and continued his conversation with the space station's dispatcher. "That might have been an accident, but it was too close for comfort. Don't bother sending out another message rocket. We can dock by ourselves."

"That is not advised, *Exedra*," the man replied. "We've got problems with our docking bays."

"I detect no problem from this range," said Aristotle, who was fiddling with the viewfinder controls. Tom believed the mechanoid's opinion rather than that of the treacherous dispatcher.

"We're coming in," he said firmly. "And try to be careful. We can't always control our comlaser. It sometimes punches holes in space stations."

He cut off the connection and smiled. "That ought to keep them honest. At least until we can dock."

"Honesty and anyone involved with Luna Corporation are strangers," Anita scoffed.

Tom expertly maneuvered the *Exedra* forward until he was within visual range of the space station. Unlike the cylindrical *New America*, it was small and doughnut-shaped to provide gravity at the rim while the center remained in zero-gee. Only a slight shudder passed through the ship as Tom nudged it into a docking berth.

"There're four other ships," Anita reported. "They've stashed them in the far loading bays. And not a one of the bays looks as if it's damaged.

The dispatcher lied to us about that."

"Of course he did," Tom grumbled.

"I can't see that they've tried hiding anything on the outside," Ben spoke up. "I've taken pictures of all their external equipment and it looks just like you'd expect." He finished the last of the photographs and stored them electronically in his computer. "And Anita's right," he added. "There's nothing wrong with any of their equipment."

"The liars," Anita grumbled.

"Since they didn't know we were coming, they didn't have time to hide anything," Tom suggested. "And whatever's causing the solar flares must be the project of this research station. So keep your eyes open. We have to find out what these people are up to."

"If we get a chance," Anita said warily. "For all we know, Luna himself might be here and meet us. And since we're not exactly friends of his, I'm not looking forward to it!"

Tom's face was grim. "I'm not either. But we have to take that chance."

Just then the airlock door opened, and everyone gasped in surprise. A pretty, blonde woman dressed in a white lab coat was waiting for them! She smiled and held out her hand.

Chapter Ten

"Welcome to *SolarSat I*," she said. "I'm Doctor Elizabeth Kerry, assistant research director."

Tom shook her hand and looked curiously into her sparkling green eyes. He had heard about Dr. Kerry and was wondering how a well-known scientist like her had come to work for David Luna. Her reputation was impeccable.

Did you know we were almost blasted out of the sky? he wanted to ask. Do you know what Luna's up to? Instead, he just mumbled a greeting.

Ben pushed forward. "Doctor Kerry, I'm honored to meet you. I've read several of your papers. But I couldn't follow all the math. Tom had to help me."

Tom laughed. "Don't believe it," he said. "Despite his modesty, Ben's an absolute whiz kid when it comes to computers."

He introduced Anita and Aristotle, sensing at once the immediate dislike Anita had for the scientist. But Dr. Kerry did not seem to be aware of it as she turned her attention to Aristotle.

"I've never seen a robot like him," she said. "He—he's almost human."

"In many ways, I am more than human," Aristotle said. "But in many others, I am a flawed mechanism. Tom has done his best with me, but I often fail him through no fault of his excellent programming."

"Tom," the woman asked, "is it possible I might borrow Aristotle for use in my research?"

"You're not going to disassemble him?" Ben asked suspiciously.

"Nothing of the sort. I need an intelligent mechanoid to run some of the more dangerous parts of our work."

"What is it you are trying to do, Doctor Kerry?" Tom asked.

"Please, call me Elizabeth." They began walking along the slightly curving corridor. On either side were laboratories filled with the most modern equipment Tom had seen since the last time he had been at Swift Enterprises on Earth.

"We're working on energy generation and

transmission," she said. "Come into my lab and I'll show you one of the experiments. Luna Corporation feels that the existing Solar Power Satellites furnishing much of Earth's electricity are outdated and far too expensive. So we're working on a bold new concept."

"I saw a null-space generator as we were docking," Tom said. "Is that part of it?"

"Yes. We're trying to open a null-space hole near the star, capture the energy radiated outward, then transmit it through null-space to a station orbiting Earth where it will be recovered. So much energy is wasted from a star. We want to utilize it."

"But opening a null-space gate inside a solar system is dangerous," Ben protested.

"Nonsense," Dr. Kerry said, with a hint of uneasiness in her tone. "There is nothing to prove that. Here, let me show you with this scale model."

On a workbench in the crammed laboratory stood a miniature null-space generator. Next to it was a simple lightbulb.

"I've never seen a generator this tiny. Why, it's hardly bigger than my fist!" Tom exclaimed.

Dr. Kerry smiled. "It's my invention. I used your basic design but miniaturized. It's not powerful enough to open too big a gateway, but for this experiment, a null-space hole the size of a pinhead will do."

"Does the lightbulb help you see what you're doing?" Anita asked sarcastically.

Doctor Kerry ignored the jibe. "Watch carefully," she said. "The gateway is activated, and then the lightbulb is turned on."

"The bulb represents the star?" Tom asked.

"Exactly." The lights in the laboratory dimmed slightly when the gateway opened. Dr. Kerry turned on the bulb, and immediately monitoring equipment on the far side of the lab began clicking and whirring.

"I see," Tom said as complete understanding came to him. "Another gateway on the other side of the lab has opened, too. The light energy is transmitted through null-space and emerges over there without any loss. Fantastic."

"Thank you. I'm proud of it. Of course, I'm more an experimental scientist than a theoretical one—"

"I understand the concept," Ben spoke up. "But could you explain your formula to me?"

"I'll be glad to," Dr. Kerry replied and pulled a set of papers out of her desk drawer. She offered the visitors seats and started to go through the theory. It was complex and took a long time, with Tom and Ben asking questions along the way.

Suddenly, after an hour or so, the lightbulb began to glow brighter and brighter. Dr. Kerry watched a moment, then spun around to hit the OFF switch. But it was too late.

The glass globe exploded into a million fragments!

She winced and turned, pulling a tiny sliver of glass from her cheek.

"It must been an old bulb," she said, her voice small.

"Was it?" Tom asked. "Or was it the first time you ran this experiment long enough? There's something about using a null-space generator in this fashion that's dangerous."

"No, it's not," she said quickly. But again, it seemed to Tom as if she were not all that convinced. "The math says it'll work."

Tom and Ben exchanged looks. Tom had developed the null-space stardrive and had an instinctive feel for it. And what Dr. Kerry described felt wrong!

"Elizabeth, is this the only research station the Luna Corporation is running?"

"Of course not. We maintain dozens of them."

"I mean research of this kind. Is there one near the Sun, our Sun?"

Before the scientist could answer, alarm bells rang all over the station.

"Another flare!" she cried. "Hurry. We've got to get behind special shielding. We're too close to the star for ordinary shields to be effective."

Tom and Ben hurried off, Aristotle trailing.

Tom glanced around. Anita had left them, evidently to explore the station on her own. He hoped the redhead would stay out of trouble.

"Mathematics can be used to show that impossible things are possible," Tom pointed out. "Have you observed any increase in solar flare activity when you open the null-space hole?"

Dr. Kerry uneasily shifted her weight from one foot to the other, then turned away before answering. "Sunspot cycles aren't predictable. We've happend to hit a peak in that activity. Coincidence, that's all."

"This is even worse than the flares hitting *New America*," Ben said tensely. "And I didn't think anything could be worse than those. They blistered the paint off the walls."

"We're a lot closer to Elira than the space colony is to the Sun," Dr. Kerry explained. "We're almost within this star's atmosphere."

"I didn't think stars had atmospheres," Ben said.

"It isn't a breathable one, like on Earth," Tom spoke up. "This one is superheated hydrogen and helium boiling at millions of degrees Kelvin."

"Turn up the air-conditioner. I'm feeling hotter just listening to you." Ben crouched behind a curving shield almost a foot thick. The others with him sat in silence, worry on their faces.

Tom looked around and saw several of the monitoring instruments. Most were giving readings hundreds of times past deadly-to-humans levels. In this radiation environment, even their robot would be in danger.

"Where's Aristotle?" he demanded. "Is he all right?"

"I am fine, Tom," came the mechanoid's voice from across the room. "I have taken refuge with the station's main computer. We are having a nice chat."

Tom smiled. Before he finished, Aristotle would have gotten every single bit of information from that computer. The robot could be very persuasive when he "spoke" with other mechanisms.

"These flares have gotten worse," Elizabeth Kerry said in a low voice. "Much worse, ever since we started regular testing."

"The math may be right," Tom pointed out, "but the concept could be wrong. We never use the *Exedra*'s stardrive within several planetary diameters because of the way null-space holes affect gravity."

"That's not the problem. I'm sure of it," the scientist said. "Our head of research is the best in the field. Tops."

"Who is that?"

"Doctor Wolfe."

"Manfred Wolfe?" Tom asked, trying to remember where he'd heard the name. Then it came to him. "He's the one CalTech fired from its staff because of slapdash experiments. He didn't take proper safety precautions and injured several graduate students."

"He wasn't responsible." Dr. Kerry defended her superior. "One of the students altered the experiment without telling him. Doctor Wolfe is a fine scientist. David Luna appreciates his genius."

"I'm sure of that," Tom snorted. "Those two have much in common. They'll do anything to achieve their goals, no matter who gets hurt."

"Mister Luna has only humankind's best interest at heart. Why else would he invest the millions required for this research?"

"Because he'll make even more millions," Ben put in. "Whoever controls cheap energy on Earth controls Earth."

Tom nodded. "Well, let's talk with Doctor Wolfe and see what his actual findings are. We might be wrong about the cause of the flares."

Dr. Kerry smiled. "Spoken like a true scientist. You don't jump to conclusions. I wish you were on the project. Clear thinking is what we need to overcome the . . . problems."

"All safe!" came the announcement over loudspeakers hung at the corners of the room. "Radiation level is back down to Elira norm."

Tom rose, stretching cramped muscles. He hadn't realized how tense he had been, crouched down behind the thick shields.

"Let's go see Doctor Wolfe," he suggested. "I'd like to hear his ideas on what causes such intense solar activity."

Dr. Kerry, Tom, and Ben walked around the perimeter of the station. The hallways had been painted a light beige to diffuse light and create a soothing environment. However, Tom felt the tension among the researchers all around him. They glanced at one another nervously, and at him as if he had come to arrest them.

"Your colleagues seem upset," Tom said to the young woman.

Elizabeth Kerry nodded slightly. "It's not your presence, if that's what you mean. Our research hasn't gone too well in some ways. I'd almost agree with you, but I trust Doctor Wolfe."

"Do you trust David Luna, too?" Tom asked.

The woman shot him a look, half angry and half frightened. She started to say something, then bit her lower lip and held it back.

"Here's Doctor Wolfe's office," she said, but Tom knew she'd intended to say something else—something concerning David Luna!

Chapter Eleven

In Dr. Wolfe's office, Elizabeth Kerry introduced Ben and Tom to the whip-thin head of *SolarSat I*. Tall and graying at the temples, the scientist presented an imposing picture of confidence and ability.

But when he heard their names, his demeanor became ice-cold.

"So you are Tom Swift," he said, a little too loudly. "I have been warned about you."

"Warned? By whom?"

"Never mind by whom. But I know you meddle in other peoples' business. I suppose you have come to spy on our project."

"I'm worried about the use of a null-space gateway so close to a star," Tom said. "The changes in gravity when the hole is opened—"

"Nonsense!" the scientist snapped. He walked around his desk. "The theory is perfect."

"Doctor Wolfe, Tom has a lot of experience with null-space drives," Elizabeth Kerry spoke up. "Perhaps you should listen to him. I myself have never been one hundred percent convinced about stellar surface stability when we open the gateway."

"If you have any doubts," Dr. Wolfe said coldly, "I suggest you quit your job."

"What if he's right?" the woman persisted.

Tom and Ben exchanged glances. She had argued for her superior earlier, but misgivings had turned her into their ally. Tom felt a surge of elation. Dr. Kerry was an accomplished scientist. Having her agree that Wolfe's calculations might not be perfect made him feel better.

"He's not right!" Wolfe insisted. "In fact, he is leaving *SolarSat I* this instant. He should never have been allowed to dock here, but . . . never mind." The man's anger cooled slightly, as he continued. "I will not have him snooping about, getting in the way, prying into Luna Corporation secrets."

"That's right, Manfred," a familiar voice came from behind them. "He's already done more than enough spying."

Tom and Ben turned to see David Luna in the

doorway. He held Anita by the wrist in a deceptively gentle manner. Tom recognized it as a judo grip. If the redhead moved suddenly, Luna could break her arm.

"I found out everything, Tom!" Anita Thorwald blurted. "This star is going nova. And they're the ones who caused it!"

"Nonsense!" Dr. Wolfe shouted. "That is only supposition."

"Engineering problems have cropped up," Luna admitted. "We're going to abandon *SolarSat I* and move our operations to *SolarSat II*."

"You can't continue with this destructive project!" Anita cried.

"Quiet, young lady." Luna tightened the grip on the girl's arm. She gasped as pain lanced into her shoulder. Luna's cold dark eyes turned to Ben as he started to come to Anita's aid. Ben froze in midstride.

"Is this true, Mister Luna?" Dr. Kerry asked. "Has the instability passed the point of no return?"

"It seems so. This star wasn't a good choice for our experiments. It was unstable when we arrived. Doctor Wolfe's theory is accurate and correct. We'll prove it on the other *SolarSat*."

"When will the star go nova?" Dr. Wolfe asked.

Luna shrugged. "Sometime soon. A few hours,

a few days. These measurements aren't precise. I've ordered the crew to begin evacuation."

Dr. Kerry's eyes widened in surprise and shock. She looked from David Luna to Tom, then back.

"I'd better tend to my section," she said, her voice shaking slightly, and left.

"I recommend you do likewise, Manfred," Luna ordered. "I'll take care of our unwanted guests."

He signalled to several men standing in the corridor. They all wore jumpsuits with the familiar Luna emblem, and silently entered the room.

"Why did you allow us to come on board?" Tom asked, stalling to give himself time to think a way out of this predicament.

The man shrugged. "It wouldn't do having you go running back to the Solar System with tall tales about our activities here. After that fool missed destroying you with the rocket, I decided to let you dock and keep an eye on you. As you see, it was a smart move on my part."

Luna grinned; then his brows furrowed. "I also found out that one of our staff members seems to have some doubts about our project," he went on, obviously referring to Dr. Kerry. "She needs watching, too!"

He gestured to the guards. "Take Swift and his

party away!" he ordered.

The men reached for the captives.

"You don't have to shove," Ben said, jerking free of one guard's grasp. "I'll go peacefully."

"Well, I won't!" Anita cried. She kicked one of the men and tried to run, but they tackled her less than ten paces down the corridor.

Tom watched helplessly. The men gripping him by the elbows were too strong to fight off!

They were taken into the central storage hub of the torus. Floating along in zero-gee would have been pleasant under other circumstances, but they were prisoners.

Tom executed a neat somersault in midair when he was tossed into the storage room. He lightly braced himself against one wall, saw his robot, and exclaimed, "Aristotle! They got you, too!"

"I did not fully understand their motives until it was too late. I am sorry, Tom. With my newly acquired knowledge of this space station, I might have successfully eluded them for many weeks."

"Don't worry about it."

"It's my fault, Tom," Anita spoke up. "I went spying in Doctor Wolfe's lab and set off an alarm. I didn't think it would be wired up. They can so easily monitor people coming into this isolated station."

"It wasn't your fault," Tom declared. "Luna was watching all of us, waiting for the proper moment to nab us. I think the only reason we stayed free as long as we did was that the solar storm interrupted him."

"We should have known Luna would be aboard," Ben grumbled. "Wherever there's trouble, he's first in line."

"Recriminations serve no purpose at this point," Aristotle said. "We naively blundered into Mister Luna's trap. We must figure out—"

"How to get out of here!" Anita interjected. "I read one of the reports saying how unstable Elira has become. Luna wasn't kidding. The instruments all showed the star will explode soon." She took a deep breath to calm herself.

"What worries me the most is Luna's mention of *SolarSat II,*" Tom said grimly.

"That particular project is in orbit around our Sun," Aristotle supplied. "I obtained this information from the space station's computer. *SolarSat II* has only been conducting start-up tests. With the addition of *SolarSat I* personnel, it can begin full-scale operation."

Tom and his friends fell silent as they thought this over. The tests of the null-space gateway David Luna had put into orbit around the Sun had already caused terrible radiation storms.

Full-time use meant the Sun would explode, just as Elira was in the process of doing!

"It looks like we have to save the world," Tom finally declared, "crazy as it may sound. And in order to do that, we have to get out of here, just as Anita said."

He floated around the storage room, hunting for a way to escape. But all the hatches were securely fastened from the outside.

While Tom was looking for an exit, Anita had an idea. She took a short connector wire she had found and hooked together the computer in her leg with Aristotle's circuitry.

"What are you up to?" Ben asked.

"I'm using Aristotle's internal electronics to monitor the radiation. And it doesn't look good. Another solar flare is building!"

"There's not much shielding in here," Ben observed. "We might be able to survive, though, if we could get back to *New America* in time for Gamma-null treatment."

"Forget it." Anita had turned white.

"What do you mean, forget it?" Ben snorted. "I don't want to be cooked by solar radiation."

"You won't," Anita said in a weak voice. "Aristotle's electronics shows the star is getting ready to explode. Not in a week—but now!"

Chapter Twelve

"They can't leave us locked up. Not when the star is going to blow up!" Benjamin Walking Eagle exclaimed.

"It seems that that is precisely what Mister Luna is doing," Aristotle stated. "Do you think he has forgotten us in the excitement?"

"No. He's probably gloating over how easy it is to get rid of us," Tom muttered.

The young inventor floated weightlessly in the center of the storage room. As he revolved slowly, his sharp eyes inventoried everything. There wasn't much. Only a few items were lying around, and they appeared useless for getting free of the metal prison.

"Tom?" Anita asked. "What will actually happen when the star explodes? What will we feel?"

"We'll never know. The first burst of radiation traveling at the speed of light would cook us instantly. The shock wave following would move a lot slower but it'd be even more devastating. Intense heat, at a temperature even hotter than the star's is now, would rush outward. Any planet in this system will be turned into vapor and blown into space."

"How cheerful," Ben mumbled. "Turned into gas and scattered across the cosmos. You always told me I was a windbag, Anita. Now it looks like you were right all along!"

"The entire system of Elira will be gone," Tom went on. "But things can be a lot worse. If our Sun explodes, there's a good possibility that its new circumference will reach out to where Mars is orbiting now."

"That's a lot of expansion," Anita said.

"When the cooling begins after this monstrous explosion, the Sun will shrink to a neutron star. Its mass will be contained in a ball only a few miles across. The Solar System will be unrecognizable."

"Earth will be vaporized," Aristotle spoke up. "The gas giants of Jupiter, Saturn, Uranus, and Neptune will be boiled away. Possibly Pluto will be a nicer place to be. All life will be gone, either from direct explosion or intense radiation."

"I don't even want to think about this!" Anita declared forcefully. "We'll have to stop Luna's mad experimentation, and the first step will be to escape from here."

"It'd take an explosion to open that door," Ben declared. "And we have no EXP-12 or even dynamite to blow the hatch."

"Explosives are too dangerous to store inside a space station," Aristotle told Ben. "I have evaluated the strength of the door. If I begin properly applying my welding torch, there is a possibility I can cut through in less than two hours."

"We don't have two hours!" Anita cried.

Just then the intercom crackled on. All three humans jumped as David Luna's taunting voice spoke to them.

"Our instruments have verified that this star is ready to blow up. Has your fabulous mechanoid also figured that out, Swift?" The man's derisive tone made Tom clench his hands into tight fists. But anger would be self-defeating.

"We know. Elira will go nova in a few hours."

"In less than an hour," David Luna corrected. "It is unfortunate that Doctor Wolfe picked an unstable star for his experiments. By transferring all our personnel to *SolarSat II*, I'm sure we can make better progress."

"No!" Tom shouted. "Don't do it. The null-space hole so near the star's surface is causing it to explode. If you start the experiments near our Sun, the same thing will happen. The Sun will go nova, too!"

"Nonsense," Luna said, contempt ringing in his voice. "Doctor Wolfe assures me his theory is right. Elira was an unstable star to begin with. We didn't study it long enough to get a good profile. The Sun is a very stable G-class star. We've already conducted preliminary tests with a new null-space gateway and the Sun does not show the same signs as Elira did."

"There were unusual solar flares. Please stop the experiment!" Tom begged. "You can kill all life if you're wrong. Do you want to be known forever by other, alien races as the madman who destroyed humanity?"

"Such a dramatic plea," Luna scoffed. "You missed your calling, Swift. You should have gone out for the theater. The delivery of the lines almost convinces me. Almost."

"How can you justify the risk?" Anita demanded. "Even if Tom has only a single chance in a million of being right, how can you continue?"

"You are making me out to be a villain. I'm not.

I'm providing humankind with cheap, clean, limitless power. There will be no more starvation, no more poverty. I will eliminate disease and create millions of new jobs."

"It will also make you even richer," Aristotle pointed out.

"True," Luna said, laughing quietly. The loudspeaker hissed and hummed as new solar flares disturbed even the space station's internal communication. "So what? I'm risking a lot of money to develop this process. I deserve the rewards."

"You'll kill everyone with this mad scheme!" Tom warned.

"I've heard enough of this, Swift. I believe Doctor Wolfe and the others. I don't believe you."

"Tom," Aristotle said, "the radiation level is rising precipitously. The shielding in this portion of the space station is currently adequate, but if new storms occur we are all in extreme danger."

"A little radiation now means nothing if we don't get out of here," Anita cried.

"Luna, let's talk about this back on Earth. Let us out and we can discuss it later," Tom pleaded.

Only hissing and crackling noises came from the speaker. Tom spun in midair, then swam gracefully over to the wall where the speaker hung.

"Luna, let us out. If you leave us here . . ." His

words trailed off. Leaving them to the fiery death throes of the star was exactly what David Luna intended. Even with his cutting torch, Aristotle could not possibly open the hatch in time.

Or could he?

Chapter Thirteen

"Tom! My sensors detect vibration through the deck plates. Luna has abandoned the space station." Aristotle spoke rapidly, continuing to run his cutting torch along the stubborn metal hinges of the door holding them inside the storage room.

Tom also had felt the ships that had been docked at the station depart. He hadn't mentioned it because he did not want to upset Ben and Anita.

"Is there anything—anything at all—we can use to escape?" he asked. If he kept the others busy, it might take their minds off their impending doom. Moreover, trying to do something, no matter how futile it seemed, was better than passively accepting their fate.

"I found a box of precision tools," Ben said. "Great for working on microcircuits but lousy for jimmying open a hatch." He turned to Aristotle and asked, "How's it coming, rust bucket?"

"I am not a rust bucket, Ben," the mechanoid answered indignantly. "Tom keeps me adequately oiled to prevent such slow oxidation of my parts. To respond to your question, progress is very slow. This is very fine 303 stainless steel. It is difficult to cut through."

"Great," Ben said. "I guess this means I'm not going to win the soda pop contest."

Tom had to smile at that. Ben's sense of humor still came through, in spite of their desperate situation.

"Have you found anything?" he asked Anita.

The redhead held up a large spatula for turning pancakes and a plastic sack filled with white powder. "Only this. Kitchen supplies. Some utensils. And almost fifty pounds of flour. If I hurry, I can mix up a batch of cookies and let the radiation bake them for us."

Tom frowned. But there was something about flour, though, that could be useful, Tom thought.

"I've got it!" he cried, amazed at his own ingenuity. "It's going to be dangerous, but it'll work. I know it."

"What?" The redhead looked at him as if he'd turned into a real space case.

"I think Tom means your cookies are dangerous. The ones I've tried were deadly," Ben joked.

"No, Ben. Listen. Do you know why grain elevators on Earth catch on fire?"

"Faulty wiring?"

"Dust," Tom replied. "As dust floats in the air, each little particle is exposed to a lot of oxygen. And there are three things needed for a fire: oxygen, fuel, and heat."

"We've got the oxygen," Ben said. "At least Luna didn't turn off the circulating fans." He pointed to tiny paper streamers billowing at the air ducts and showing that the space station's atmosphere still circulated.

"We also have the heat," Aristotle spoke up. He turned on his motorframe and thrust out the blue-white tongue of flame hissing from his cutting torch.

"And the flour," Tom said excitedly, "will be our fuel! Grain elevators explode because the dust gets in the air and static electricity ignites it. Whoosh! Up goes the entire building. We can duplicate it."

Aristotle faced Tom.

"If I understand your plan, this will require the air circulation equipment to be turned off to prevent the burning flour motes from being blown out. But the switches are outside in the main portion of the station, beyond our reach."

"Weld plates over the air ducts!"

"Tom, are you sure about this?" Ben asked uneasily. "If you cut off our air, we'll suffocate."

"This will work. I know it." Tom didn't add that there'd hardly be any time for any of them to suffocate. The exploding star would turn them to cinders long before that could happen.

Aristotle went to work. "The air ducts are closed," he reported a few moments later. "May I suggest using my body to shield you three from the effects of the explosion?"

"Thanks, Aristotle." Tom pulled crates around and piled them directly in front of the hatch to direct the blast outward as much as possible, then nodded to Anita. She ripped open bag after bag of flour. The white dust rippled and flowed through the air, hanging in zero-gee until it formed a cloud as dense as any fog on Earth.

"Turn on your cutting torch again, Aristotle," Tom ordered. "And brace yourselves, everyone!"

The mechanoid flipped on the electric spark igniter. The result was a thousand times more violent than any of them had expected. The flour particles each caught fire and burned rapidly. The rush to suck up ever more oxygen and expand caused an explosion that blasted the hatch off the storeroom and sent it rocketing down the corridor.

"Are you all right?" Aristotle asked anxiously. He stood over the three dazed humans.

For several seconds, Tom could only nod. The ringing in his ears slowly went away and he floated upward, glad he didn't have to walk. His legs felt shaky.

"It worked," he whispered. "It worked!"

"There was never any doubt in my central processing unit," Aristotle assured him. "This was a clever application of the laws of physics."

"Let's not waste any time congratulating ourselves," Tom urged. "We've got to get to the *Exedra* and get away from here."

Ben, Anita, and Tom swam forward through the air, as if they were in water, then felt the slight tug of artificial gravity as they came closer to the space station's outer ring.

"It's good to feel weight again." Ben sighed in obvious relief. "In fact, it's good to feel anything."

"Where *is* everyone?" Anita asked. "They couldn't all have gone already!"

"Luna can be very efficient," Tom said. "He's an expert at organization."

"It almost sounds as if you admire the man," Ben chuckled.

"I do admire his abilities," Tom said. "In his own way, he's a genius. Too bad he's an evil one." He stopped for a moment and looked around.

"Come on," Ben urged. "There's no time for sightseeing now."

"I know, but I want to be sure that everyone has left. We ought to check."

"We might miss our flight if we do!" Anita pointed out.

"I know. What do you think?"

Anita sighed. "I guess we check."

"Okay. Look into every compartment, every lab," Tom said. "Make sure everyone's out. I'll try the infirmary. A patient may be bedridden. Ben, look in the storerooms. I don't think Luna had anyone else imprisoned, but we have to be certain."

He paused, then added, "Aristotle, plug into the central computer and monitor all available security cameras and loudspeakers throughout the station. Someone might be able to contact us that way."

"Yes, Tom." The mechanoid turned and rolled away.

The friends split up, intent on their missions. Tom ran quickly along corridors strewn with debris that had been discarded as the station crew fled. He hastily glanced into every lab, listened for sounds, then hurried on. He panted from exertion by the time he had circled the large outer ring of *SolarSat I*.

He'd found that no one was left behind.

"Nothing, Tom," Ben reported.

Anita carried several cages packed with rabbits and white mice. "No humans, but a lot of life," she declared.

"Bring them along," Tom said, smiling. "We've got the room aboard ship."

"We must hurry," Aristotle said. "My linkage with the station's computer and its more extensive instrumentation indicates growing turbulence on Elira's surface. Some enormous sunspots have begun to form. These relatively cool areas create further disruption in the star's thermonuclear cycle."

"We're leaving," Tom agreed. "We've done all we can."

"Good," the mechanoid said. "My monitoring shows that a nova condition will occur within the hour. Perhaps even less time remains for us. The star has reached a critical point in its stellar evolution."

The trio raced off, clutching cages of chattering, frightened animals. Aristotle whirred along behind. They reached the outer docking area, out of breath from their exertion.

"Start the airlock cycle, Ben," Tom ordered. "I'll check out the—oh, no!" The young inventor stared out the glassite porthole in disbelief.

"What is it?" Anita asked. "They haven't wrecked the *Exedra*, have they?"

"Worse. They have taken it. And all the other shuttles and starships are gone, too. Luna not only locked us in the storeroom, he trapped us on the station!"

Chapter Fourteen

"Spacesuits!" Ben shouted. "We can get into spacesuits and—"

"Forget it," Tom said. "Spacesuits won't do us any good."

"If we can jettison a part of the station," Anita exclaimed, "and then use it for a spaceship hull, we can get away." She warmed to her far-out idea, getting more enthusiastic. "We can attach small chemical rockets on the outer rim. Then we blast ourselves away. We could do something like you and Aristotle did back on *New America* when the lab nodule was cut loose."

"Anita, my calculations show that the star will go nova in less than ten minutes," Aristotle said. 111

"Even if your scheme were practical, we do not have enough time to carry it out."

The mechanoid's eyes were blinking on and off balefully, and his obvious sorrow at their end was felt by all three humans. It proved to them that Aristotle was truly more than a mere collection of circuits.

From deep inside the space station came the loud clanging of alarm bells. Red lights flashed, warning of rising radiation levels. Their time was running out too fast for any scheme Tom might think up!

He turned and leaned heavily against the radar unit used to guide in ships during docking. Suddenly he saw a movement on the pale green, glowing radar screen.

"A blip!" he yelled. "There's a spaceship coming back to the station!"

A familiar voice came from the speaker overhead. "Hello, Swift party. Are you there? Over."

"Doctor Kerry, we're here!" Ben radioed back enthusiastically. "We got out of the storeroom, but Luna has taken our ship."

"I know. I'm piloting the *Exedra*. Get the docking bay ready."

"Hurry," Tom urged, speaking over Ben's shoulder. "Aristotle says that Elira will go nova in less than ten minutes."

"I know," came the strained reply. "My calculations show the same."

Tom watched as the scientist expertly brought the *Exedra* in for docking. There wasn't a single wasted motion, or a single lost moment. When the airlock began to cycle open, Anita hurried forward, carrying the cages of the small lab animals.

"Everybody in," Tom ordered. He didn't have to tell them twice. Ben raced like the wind for the computers in the cockpit. Aristotle whirred by and Tom closed the airlock.

"Only minutes remain before the star erupts," the robot announced. "There is not enough time to enter null-space."

It was true. Even as Tom ran for the cockpit, his mind worked on a flight plan. The *Exedra* had to reach a certain velocity before the stardrive worked. Using the rocket engines to reach this velocity took time they didn't have. Besides, going into stardrive too near the planet would trigger its explosion.

"What are we going to do, Tom?" Elizabeth Kerry shifted to the copilot's seat, allowing Tom access to the main control panel. "We can't possibly build up enough speed to escape the shock wave when Elira explodes."

"There's a way," Tom said. "What happens first

when a star goes nova?"

"Lots of radiation is released," Dr. Kerry responded. "Photons, X-rays, radiation from up and down the electromagnetic spectrum, and all traveling at the speed of light."

"Right," Tom agreed. "I've been working on a set of solar sails to trap photons and push the *Exedra* along like a boat uses sails on the water."

"Tom!" Ben called. "All I'm getting out of the computer is one long, constant danger signal. Every instrument is reading maximum! Some of them are even overloading!"

"Deploy sunsails," Tom called out to Anita. He didn't have to tell her to hurry. On either side of the starship sprouted long, slender aluminum arms. From the arms grew gauze-thin fabric until a complete circle around the center of the ship was completed.

"Elira's exploded!" Ben cried from his post at the computer.

The starship shuddered under the instant impact of radiation. Under normal circumstances, the *Exedra* would have ridden the solar wind at a gradually increasing speed. Not now. It felt as if a giant fist grabbed the spaceship, then cast it away.

"It's like being caught in a hurricane!" Elizabeth Kerry exclaimed. "But we're riding the light-speed waves and staying ahead of the destructive shock waves. We'll make it, Tom, we'll make it!"

Tom smiled at the woman's encouraging words. He felt happy that another invention of his had worked—and in time to save their lives. Without the sunsails, the *Exedra* could never have accelerated fast enough to escape the deadly curtain of superheated gases rushing outward at only a bit less than the speed of light.

"Aristotle, are we up to velocity for the null-space drive to work?" he asked after a while. "I don't want to stay around a second longer than necessary." He glanced in the visual monitor overhead showing Elira. Only violent, blinding light met his blue eyes.

"All ready," Aristotle stated.

"Let's hit it, then." Tom's finger stabbed the proper button. The computers worked quickly to plot the course back home to the Solar System and everything reversed. Tom gasped when the shock of entering null-space seized hold of his senses. The inside-out feeling made him dizzy and disoriented.

He was glad when the stardrive ceased and the sensation went away.

"That's the Sun straight ahead!" Ben called out. "All the computers agree. We're a bit far out, maybe, but nothing too drastic."

Only then did Tom let out a sigh of relief and lean back in his contoured seat.

Anita's voice carried a lot of emotion when she said, "I'm glad that's all over!" She came forward and stood next to Dr. Kerry's chair.

"I misjudged you, Elizabeth. I thought you were like Manfred Wolfe and David Luna. You didn't have to risk your life to save us, but you did. That took a lot of courage. Thanks."

"I couldn't let you die!" Elizabeth said.

"Did you know Luna fired a rocket at us before we landed?" Anita questioned.

"No. I heard about the rivalry between Tom and Luna, but I had no idea that Luna would go to such extremes. When I heard you were coming aboard our station, I came to talk to you because I had doubts about our project."

"Were you the only one?" Ben asked.

"There were a few others, but none of us were sure whether we were right and Luna was wrong."

"Why didn't you and the others simply stop working and ask to be sent back to Earth?" Ben asked. "You could have notified the authorities about the project and the danger it caused."

"One man asked for a transfer and was told that none would be granted until our work on

SolarSat I was over."

"You were practically his prisoners," Tom said grimly.

"Right. I was hoping you'd pick up enough information and go back to *New America* and evaluate it. That was before I heard he tried to kill you before you even landed."

Dr. Kerry pushed a strand of blonde hair out of her face before she continued.

"When I had taken care of everything and everyone in my department, I saw Luna and Doctor Wolfe boarding Luna's private yacht."

"The *Giannini?*" Tom put in. "I know it. It's a good ship. They wouldn't have had any troubles escaping in it."

"Right. But you weren't with them. I inquired whether you were on any of the other spaceships and found out you were not. So I took off in the *Exedra* and then doubled back after everyone had gone."

"David Luna may be ruthless but he sure had some good people working for him this time," Ben said. "And Doctor Kerry has my vote for being one of the best!"

"Seconded!" Anita, Tom, and Aristotle chimed in.

Tears formed at the corners of the woman's

brilliant green eyes. She dabbed them away gently.

"That's one of the nicest things anyone's ever said to me. Being friends with all of you means a lot."

"Let's plot a course back for Earth," Tom said. "Living in space is fine, but I need to see a nice green, brown, and blue planet now and then."

They quickly laid out the course and started toward the Sun. Ben worked on the computers. "There's something I don't understand," he spoke up.

"What's that?" Tom asked.

"When I plotted the course to Elira, I took a spectrographic reading. I just checked and the star's spectrum is still the same as when we left. But Elira's blown up so the spectrum ought to be different."

"Ben," Elizabeth answered, "you're forgetting the speed of light. It'll take years for the light from the explosion to reach Earth. We got around that time delay by ducking in and out of null-space."

"Of course!" the Indian exclaimed, whacking himself on the forehead with the palm of his hand. "How could I forget?"

"We've all been under a big strain," Tom said.

"And that's not going to change," Elizabeth

predicted grimly. "Don't forget Luna has *SolarSat II* orbiting the Sun. When he and Doctor Wolfe turn on the null-space gateway, they're going to repeat the Elira disaster!"

They all were silent as they stared out the inch-thick glassite port at the tiny dot of the Sun. They'd reentered the Solar System beyond Jupiter's orbit. With rocket drives at full blast, it would take them over two weeks to reach *New America*.

"Can't we speed up our trip using the sunsails?" Anita asked.

"Unlike a boat, which uses water for friction to tack into the wind, the *Exedra* has only empty space around it," Aristotle explained. "It is possible to 'tack' into the solar wind but Tom has not yet outfitted the *Exedra* with such magnetic running boards."

Tom nodded. "So it's rockets all the way," he said. "I think I'll spend the time running some tests in the lab."

"And we girls can soak in our super spatial bathtub!" Anita chuckled as she turned to the scientist. "When Tom converted the *Exedra* from the luxury yacht it once was, Elizabeth, I talked him into keeping the tub. It's just great!"

Ben smiled. "We'll have a fun trip home, eh? Well, I can use some rest. Maybe I'll come up with the winning name for the soda pop."

Tom was happy about the budding friendship between Anita and Elizabeth. He'd let them relax for a while before they resumed the serious work ahead.

The two went off to tend to the animals Anita had brought on board. Ben offered to help, leaving Tom to sit and stare through the viewport into the velvet blackness of space.

But it wasn't emptiness he saw. He imagined David Luna's diabolical *SolarSat II* orbiting the Sun. With its null-space hole levered open to transport energy, the Sun's surface churned and boiled with unnatural activity. Tom Swift then envisioned the entire Sun blasting apart, killing all life within the Solar System.

He had to stop Luna before that happened. He had to!

Chapter Fifteen

"It's growing worse by the day—by the hour." Dr. Kerry shook her head, a soft halo of golden blonde hair drifting around her lovely face. "There isn't any doubt now. I've checked it every day for the past week and a half. Our Sun is acting the same way Elira did just before it went nova."

"The Sun's going to explode." Ben Walking Eagle uttered the words in a flat, emotionless voice. "We kind of expected it, but now we're sure."

"That's correct."

"We can stop David Luna," Anita said firmly. "We're done it in the past. His greed makes him careless. His mistakes always trip him up. Right, Tom?"

The young inventor didn't answer right away. He finished off a series of quick calculations before speaking.

"Sure, we've played on Luna's weaknesses before. Some skill was involved, but in the past we've also been lucky. But it doesn't look like we're going to have a shot at it this time."

"What do you mean?"

"*SolarSat II* is on the other side of the Sun. Even if we could get through the static produced by the solar flares and talk to my father, no one on Earth could reach the place in time to stop him."

"That's right," Doctor Kerry confirmed. "*SolarSat II* circles inside Mercury's orbit. It takes Mercury eighty-eight days to revolve around the Sun. The research station's 'year' is only slightly longer than seventy-one days. It was just starting behind the Sun relative to our position when we reentered the Solar System."

"So we'd have to wait a half *SolarSat* 'year,' or thirty-six days, for the space station to come back to this side," Ben said slowly, understanding the problem. "Only we don't have a month to spare!"

"So there's not a thing we can do," Anita muttered. "Absolutely nothing."

"Maybe there is," Aristotle spoke up.

"What do you mean?" Tom asked eagerly, turning to look at the mechanoid.

Aristotle's eyes flashed off and on in mechanical excitement.

"I have talked a great deal with the ship's computer. One orbit will let us arrive in less than the time Doctor Kerry predicts for the Sun to go nova."

"Show me the orbit!" Tom cried. "Why didn't I try working through all of them myself? What a fool I've been!"

"The orbit is dangerous," Aristotle warned.

Tom scanned the numbers, verified Aristotle's calculations with a quick computer check of his own, then sagged.

"It *is* dangerous," he said. "We'd have to enter the Sun's photosphere and swing closer to the surface than anyone's ever gone before. Not even unmanned probes have survived that close to the Sun. The temperature is millions of degrees."

"You mean this is the only orbit that would get us to *SolarSat II*, and if we followed it, we'd end up like boiled lobsters?" Ben grunted. The way he crossed his arms over his broad chest told of his disappointment.

"Why don't we use the null-space drive?" Anita said. "We've nothing to lose. We warp out to a point on the other side, then use the null-space drive to get in close."

Dr. Kerry shook her head at the girl's suggestion. "It wouldn't work. It would trigger the nova. We'd be causing what we want to avoid."

"We have to rethink the problem," Tom said. "Until we come up with a better solution, I'm turning on the rockets full blast along the course Aristotle has computed for us."

As he did, the *Exedra* lurched, and everyone on board felt heavy due to the acceleration.

"I weigh a million tons now," Anita complained. "What good does it do to diet if you just make me weigh even more?"

Tom had to laugh. Anita Thorwald didn't need to diet at all. Her figure was kept trim by exercise and staying active all the time, yet she worried about the slightest amounts of unwanted bulge.

"Maybe that's the approach to use," Ben mumbled.

"What approach? Tell us," demanded the redhead.

"I'll not only name the soda pop, I'll give a slogan to go along with it. 'Drink Accelo-Pop. It goes down heavy.'"

Anita threw a book at Ben, but missed, not taking into account the added weight due to the acceleration. He laughed in delight, the strain momentarily broken.

Tom turned his attention back to the problem confronting them. How could they get rid of the heat? *New America* used extensive radiation fins on the exterior, but the *Exedra* had nothing like that. He did some figuring and determined that the ship's air-conditioning system, even working at full capacity, wouldn't keep the interior temperature below boiling.

He gazed out the glassite port. The Sun grew in size minute by minute. It was dimmed by the heavy polarizing filter he had installed over the window, but the disk was still so bright that it made the young inventor squint. Soon he'd have to shutter the viewport entirely.

"Tom," Anita spoke up. "There must be something you can do. Is there any invention you have been working on that might help us now?"

"I haven't had much chance to develop anything lately besides the sunsails. I haven't really done anything since—Aristotle!" he cried. "How could I have missed it! It's obvious. The Shadowlator!"

"What's that?" Dr. Kerry asked.

"It's a device that alters the molecular structure of any material within its field," Tom explained, "in order to allow light waves to pass through. When it's in operation, only a ghostly outline of an object can be seen."

"I do not understand how this will be of any help," Aristotle spoke up.

"Light is radiation," Tom explained. "Heat is

radiation, too, but with a much longer wavelength. If I use the Shadowlator and tune it for the longer heat waves, it'll let them pass right through, keeping the ship from getting too hot. The air-conditioning unit can probably keep the inside cool enough if the Shadowlator is able to help out."

"An excellent idea. I have begun calculations to see if this will be sufficient." Aristotle stood for a moment, quietly humming to himself. When his eyes flashed a bright green, he almost seemed to smile in a human fashion. "It *will* work, Tom! It will work nicely."

Sweat poured from Tom's forehead by the time he finished making the delicate adjustments needed to the frequency controls on his Shadowlator. He sat back in satisfaction, looking up at the mechanoid.

"Here it goes, old buddy. And just in time, too!"

With the others watching tensely, he flipped the switch activating the Shadowlator's field. For a moment nothing happened; then everything shimmered before his eyes. Tom blinked rapidly and relaxed. He felt an immediate reduction in temperature inside the ship. The heat passed straight through, no longer heating the metal of the ship.

"It's working!" Dr. Kerry cried. "The air-conditioning is able to keep us cool."

"We are still over twenty million miles from the Sun," Aristotle warned. "It will get much, much warmer yet."

They watched as the Sun grew larger and brighter by the minute.

"This is the last direct look we're going to get," Tom said. "I'm closing the shutter until we reach the other side."

As he did, he felt a deep shuddering vibration pass through the ship. Worried, he checked the control panel.

"Aristotle!" he cried. "Ben! The Shadowlator's malfunctioning. Check out all the circuits, quick!"

A few moments later, Ben's anguished reply came. "I've got it, Tom. The Shadowlator is taking away too much energy from the main power units. The air-conditioning and the controllers on the rockets have first priority. As a result, the Shadowlator is shutting itself off to keep the other systems operating."

"If energy is all you need," Aristotle said, "why not make use of solar cells? I believe you still have a few aboard. They could be placed on the exterior of the ship and provide added power to the Shadowlator."

"That's it!" Tom cried. "The Solar Power Satellites around Earth use large banks of solar cells. So can we! And we're almost on top of the Sun. We ought to get that much more electricity out of the cells."

"But they'd have to be put on the outer hull," Dr. Kerry protested. "This close to the Sun makes going outside very dangerous, even for Aristotle."

"Not if I roll the ship so that the airlock is facing away from the Sun," Tom declared. "I can go out and do it myself, as long as the ship blocks out the radiation. It won't take ten minutes."

"It'll be close," Ben said. "We have to keep the *Exedra* rolling to prevent one side from heating up faster than the other. If that happens, we start to melt things inside, air-conditioning or not."

Elizabeth and Anita immediately spoke up, demanding to help.

"Doctor Kerry is a better pilot than I am," Anita said quickly, cutting off the scientist's arguments. "I don't have anything to do aboard, so I'm going. And you can't stop me."

"I don't have time to argue," Tom said.

"Two can get the work done twice as fast," she pointed out.

"All right," he said reluctantly.

By the time they reached the airlock, Aristotle had assembled two massive arrays of the silicon chips that converted sunlight directly into electricity.

"I shall begin work on the connections inside, Tom," the mechanoid informed him. "Please hurry. There is little time before it becomes too hot for humans inside the ship."

"Okay."

Tom signaled Ben to stop the *Exedra*'s slow rotation. When the airlock was directly away from the Sun, he and Anita swung out. For a giddy moment, Tom felt as if he floated in empty space.

The Shadowlator worked only occasionally, making it appear as if the *Exedra* winked on and off.

"Over there, Anita. Start the solar cells from that bracket and I'll get this array put into place here." The static caused by nearness to the Sun made radio communication, even at this short distance, almost impossible. But Anita knew what to do. She worked quickly and well, finishing a few seconds before Tom.

He checked to make sure that the solar cells were properly fastened and all electrical connections secured. Only then did he swing back into the airlock after Anita.

As soon as the hatch closed and air filled the small room, he unfastened his helmet and called out to Aristotle, "Switch on the Shadowlator!"

Chapter Sixteen

The temperature dropped a few precious degrees. But that was all.

Tom slipped into the pilot's chair and studied the readouts. The ship was within ten million miles of the Sun—still nine million miles from their closest approach. The heat inside the *Exedra* stifled him, making it hard to breathe.

"Turn off everything that's not essential," he ordered his crew. "Keep the air-conditioner, the Shadowlator, and the engine controls running. Everything else must be shut down."

This helped—for a while. Some time later, Ben said in a choked voice, "Cabin temperature is one

hundred and thirty. The Shadowlator is not

keeping it as cool as we thought it would."

"It's still about forty degrees under what we'd have without it," Tom said. "We'll make it. We have to. Just take it easy. Everything's on automatic."

The controls wavered in front of him. He didn't know if that was because of heat shimmer like that seen in deserts or if he was blacking out.

"Two million miles from the Sun," Aristotle announced. "Cabin temperature one hundred and thirty-five."

Tom blinked the sweat from his eyes. He felt too drained to reach up and brush the moisture away with his hand. This was as close to the Sun as anyone had ever come. Tongues of flames caressed the hull of the *Exedra*. Intense gravity pulled him deep into the cushions on his couch. And the heat built . . . and built . . . and built.

Finally Tom passed out.

Visions of steamy waterfalls danced in his head. He moaned and tried to roll over. Pain seared his body, bringing him back to a state of awareness. The air felt as if he'd been dropped into a hot sponge.

Then he understood.

He was alive!

"Aristotle!" he called out.

"I am glad to see you are conscious again," the

mechanoid said. "All is well with the *Exedra*. A few minor systems did not survive. I fear Anita will have to do without her bathtub for some time. The water trapped in the pipes leading to the tub began to boil. Several of those pipes burst. It will require many hours of work to replace them. Much of the released water has gone into our air system, causing this high humidity."

"How about the others? Are they all right?" Tom demanded.

"Ben is fine. Anita and Elizabeth survived in even better shape. They seem more resistant to heat than either you or Ben."

Tom struggled to sit up. He swam in a pool of his own perspiration, but never had he felt better. They'd challenged the Sun and triumphed!

"Wow, I must have passed out for quite a while. We're already twenty million miles on the other side."

"Yes. I have located *SolarSat II*," the mechanoid went on proudly. "It is less than an hour's flight away. I have not attempted to contact the research station, believing you would want that honor."

"Thanks, Aristotle. I don't know what we'd do without you."

He thought for a moment, then turned to Dr. Kerry. "Elizabeth?"

"Yes. I'm fine, Tom."

"Good. Listen, do you think it'd do any good for *you* to contact the research station? They might listen to you."

The scientist nodded. "They'll probably shut off the radio if they hear your voice. And I worked well with Doctor Wolfe, even if we did have our disagreements. I could try."

"They might fire on us, even if Elizabeth contacts them," Ben warned. "After all, Luna tried to kill us on *SolarSat I*."

"They don't know we're alive," Anita pointed out. "Luna thinks we were killed when Elira exploded. I say, let's rush on up and board and take 'em before they know what's happening."

Tom sat back, thinking hard. He finally shook his head. "That won't work. They'd detect us and, as Ben said, would fire at us."

"Tom," the mechanoid spoke up, "may I make a suggestion?" After the young inventor nodded, Aristotle continued. "The Shadowlator can be readjusted to make us invisible to their radar. If you do that, we might be able to sneak up on them as Anita suggests."

"The ship might be invisible to their radar, but a visual sighting is still possible," Tom pointed out.

"But we're coming in from the direction of the

Sun!" Ben exclaimed. "We would vanish in the glare—and they sure won't expect us to come from that direction!"

Tom grinned. "Okay. It's worth a try," he said.

After the Shadowlator was adjusted to allow all radar beams to pass through, Tom swung the *Exedra* around so that the Sun blazed brightly behind. The tiny dot of *SolarSat II* gleamed ahead. He slowly jockeyed for position, sneaking up on the station.

For a time, he thought they'd make it. Then, suddenly, tiny flashes of light came from either side of the space station.

"Missiles!" Ben cried. "Heading for us! How did they sight us?"

"How can we avoid the missiles?" Tom mumbled. His fingers danced over the controls, turning the *Exedra* on its tail and sending power flooding through the immense engines. The acceleration pressed them all into their couches.

"The missiles are going past us! They missed by miles!" Ben crowed.

"I figured they might be heat-seekers. I got out of the way and let them lock on to the Sun. Is the station equipped with combat lasers, Elizabeth?" he asked worriedly.

"It is," Dr. Kerry said in a choked voice. "They use the high-power lasers for tests on the null-space gateway."

"There, on the top of the station," Anita cried. "I see one. And it's turning in our direction!"

Tom worked frantically at the Shadowlator controls. A lance of pure light stabbed forth from the laser, grazing the side of the *Exedra*. The entire ship shuddered in reaction.

"They blew away our portside escape nodules. Only one remains on the right side," Anita reported.

"Tom, we can't survive another hit," Dr. Kerry cried.

"We may not have to take another hit."

"They fired again. Right on target!"

The beam of potent light reached the *Exedra*, then slipped right on through the length of the ship. All inside sat for a moment, blinking.

"The Shadowlator!" Ben said in relief. "You tuned it for the laser's frequency, didn't you, Tom?"

The blond inventor nodded, then said, "We've got to get on board the station fast. Elizabeth, are there others who might agree to halt the tests and aid us?"

"Yes, there are some who would listen. Not all of them are as unfeeling and insensitive as Mister Luna."

The interference from the Sun produced an ear-shattering screech when Ben turned on the radio, but a few minutes' work with his computers filtered out much of the noise. Elizabeth took a deep breath to steady her nerves and touched the button allowing her to transmit.

"This is Doctor Kerry," she began. "Come in, *SolarSat II*. I have a message of the utmost importance."

"Doctor Kerry?" came the hesitant reply. "This is Jimmy Nnamdi. We all thought you were dead, lost in the nova, until Luna ordered the missiles and laser to fire on your ship. How'd you avoid the laser? That was great!"

"Jimmy," the woman said with relief, "Tom Swift and his friends saw to that. Now listen, you're on the technical staff. How many others would support you in a mutiny?"

"Enough," came the man's immediate reply. "But it doesn't look good. Doctor Wolfe isn't rational, and Luna still insists this project will work. A lot of the people will follow him, no matter what. Some of us have already begun sabotaging the project, though. We've seen the results. We don't understand what's going on, but it's obvious to us that we're causing it somehow."

"Tom believes the null-space gateway causes the Sun's instability. I think he's right. Look at the data and see if you don't agree with us. Then *shut down the null-space gate*! The entire Solar System depends on it."

Heavy interference caused Ben to turn down the volume on the speaker. The roar coming out of it almost deafened them. Any reply Jimmy Nnamdi might have made was lost in the sea of static.

"Jimmy is one of the best technicians on the *SolarSat* project," Elizabeth explained. "If I had to pick a single person to act responsibly, he'd be the one."

"Let's hope he has the chance," Anita said with feeling.

"How close are we to the space station, Ben?" Tom asked.

"Less than a hundred miles. I've left the Shadowlator on so that they won't be able to nail us easily with that laser. But they definitely know we're coming."

Tom worked to bring the ship in under the space station in such a way that no more missiles could be fired at them. Only occasional bursts from the laser tried to skewer them, and these passed harmlessly through the ship, thanks to the Shadowlator.

"Doctor Kerry?" came a voice out of the radio. Tom tensed, recognizing the sarcastic tone. "This is David Luna. I do not appreciate your trying to incite mutiny in my crew. There are strict laws about that."

"Mister Luna," the woman shouted. "Turn off the null-space gateway. It's upsetting the delicate balance of the Sun. Please! Even if you don't believe it's dangerous, just turn it off for a while."

A cold laugh echoed from the speaker. "I will do no such thing!"

Chapter Seventeen

Dr. Kerry's face fell as if she had given up all hope. Luna's voice kept coming over the radio.

"You and Swift are conspiring to steal my invention for yourselves," he went on. "Manfred Wolfe and I are putting the finishing touches on the null-space generator now. In a very short time we will have it operating at full power. Do not try to board the station or you'll be sorry."

A pop signaled the end of the conversation. Elizabeth slumped forward, her head down. Tom reached over and touched her lightly on the arm, reassuring her.

"We'll stop him. We haven't come this far to turn around and go home like whipped dogs." 139

"There's one thing in our favor," Elizabeth responded. "*SolarSat II* isn't equipped to stop us from boarding. Such equipment was too costly to install this close to the Sun."

"Then let's go in and stop them!" Anita cried. "David Luna won't stand a change against all of us!"

Tom had to admire the girls' enthusiasm and determination, but he knew boarding the research station would be much more difficult than it sounded. If Luna or Dr. Wolfe decided to weld shut the airlock doors, getting aboard presented big problems.

"They are opening the null-space gate. All my sensors detect it," Aristotle said. "We must hurry. If it is operational at this level for more than five minutes, the Sun will never be able to recover its stability. It will go nova as Elira has done."

"You're a cheerful one," Ben muttered.

"I am only providing an accurate appraisal of the situation confronting us," Aristotle said haughtily.

Tom didn't listen to the banter. He concentrated totally on docking next to the research station. It wasn't his best landing. The *Exedra* hit too hard and sent a jolt throughout the ship that rattled their teeth.

"Get into the station," Tom urged his friends.

He made sure that the *Exedra* was secure, but ready to blast off at an instant's notice. Then he raced after the others.

By the time he reached the airlock, he found a free-for-all in progress. The crew Luna had sent to weld shut the airlock had been ambushed by a small group of mutineers, and the new arrivals had joined in.

Ben and two men in lab coats fought near the door. Tom rushed forward and tackled the nearest one. This allowed his friend to shove the other into the next room and slam and lock the door behind him.

When Ben saw Tom struggling with one of his attackers, he took on the man. "I'll take care of him," he called out. "Tom, you go find Anita and Elizabeth. They went after Luna!"

Tom scrambled to his feet, all too aware of the time running out. According to Aristotle, they had a few minutes before the Sun reached the point of no return. By then the gate had to be turned off. Valuable moments had already passed in docking and fighting their way in. They had to succeed!

"Tom, here!" Elizabeth Kerry called just then.

He punched his opponent in the jaw, then spun and ran down the corridor. Anita pounded her fists against a locked door in a side hallway.

Other mutineers crowded around her.

"Luna and Doctor Wolfe are in the control room," she cried. "They've turned on the null-space gate at full power!"

"We can't knock this door down," Tom shouted. "It's too thick. Does anyone have a key?"

"I do!" a black man in a lab coat replied. "After I talked to Doctor Kerry, I got the master key. I'm Jimmy Nnamdi. Here, let me by." The technician sidled past the group and thrust a slender metal rod into the lock. Electronic impulses were exchanged between key and locking device, were approved, and the door opened.

David Luna whirled around and faced the intruders. "Stand back!" he bellowed. "We won't allow you to meddle in this project. It's too important."

Tom ignored him and addressed Manfred Wolfe.

"Doctor Wolfe," he said, "reconsider. You might be wrong. The evidence is against your theory, no matter how precise the math looks. The Sun is going to explode and you're causing it!"

"Don't listen, Manfred," Luna said in his cold voice. "They want to rob you of the honor of being the man in charge of the greatest humanitarian project in history. They want to steal the glory—*your* well-deserved glory."

"Doctor Wolfe, listen to me," Elizabeth Kerry pleaded. "A few minutes more isn't going to matter."

"They're taking over the station," Luna hissed. "There were traitors throughout the ranks. Like that one!" He pointed to Jimmy.

"Not traitors, just people who have doubts." Elizabeth advanced on the director of research. Dr. Wolfe looked drawn and tired, and his nerves seemed stretched to the breaking point.

"I don't know what's right. The math says I am. But what if I'm wrong?" he cried out.

Tom saw that the stress had unbalanced Wolfe, who began to shake. Luna had obviously played on that weakness.

"Trust us," Tom said. "Shut down the null-space gateway."

He and Anita signaled to each other, then shot forward as a team. Anita blocked David Luna to give Tom the time to force Dr. Wolfe away from the controls. Elizabeth quickly worked on the switches and turned off the generator.

From deep within the station, they heard a humming rise in pitch, then slowly vanish. The hole in space causing all the trouble had been closed!

"Wow, I'm glad this is over," Tom said, relieved. Then he looked up and saw Dr. Kerry's pale face turn even whiter.

"It's all over, Tom, but not the way you meant," Elizabeth said in a choked voice. "The gateway was in operation too long. We weren't in time to stop the Sun from going nova."

"No!" he cried, but quickly realized she was right. No matter how he checked the instruments, the conclusion was the same.

The Sun was in the beginning stages of exploding. No power on Earth could stop it now. The huge ball of gas would heat, expand, and erupt with a violence unknown to any living being.

The Solar System would be destroyed in one fiery burst.

"There is no mistake, Tom." Aristotle had double-checked the results. "The Sun will explode in less than one day. I only wish I could have prevented such a catastrophe. But I am a flawed mechanism and I have failed!"

"You did everything you could, Aristotle. We all did," Tom said glumly.

"Why are you getting so upset, Swift?" David Luna rasped. "You're wrong about the Sun blowing up. You have to be. Tell them, Doctor Wolfe."

Manfred Wolfe was in no condition to defend Luna's position. He sat in the corner of the control room and moaned softly to himself. The only movement he seemed capable of was a gentle rocking back and forth.

"The shock's unhinged him, Luna," Ben said. "That alone ought to show you how wrong you are. You'll be responsible for killing every man, woman, and child in the human race. How will it feel to be the biggest murderer in history?" He advanced on Luna, fists clenched.

Tom restrained his friend. "It won't do any good. The damage is done."

David Luna, for the first time, looked apprehensive. "You're not sure about the Sun exploding. You can't be."

"We can only be absolutely positive after it happens. But then it'll be too late," Tom said in a grim voice.

"It's even worse than I first imagined," Dr. Kerry spoke up. "The Sun is now generating so much excess energy that this station is in immediate danger. We're going to have to evacuate or be cooked."

SolarSat II orbited the sun at a distance of thirty million miles, over six million miles inside the planet Mercury's orbit. Tom considered evacuation to Mercury, then decided against it. The best course lay in getting the crew aboard their ships and heading them straight for Earth.

"Who is the most capable person we can put in

charge of the evacuation?" he asked Elizabeth.

"Jimmy Nnamdi. He's able to think on his own and doesn't have to be told every little thing. He organized the mutiny at just the right time for us, too. Without him, we'd never have been able to get into the station."

Jimmy smiled broadly at the confidence that was placed in him.

"Can you get everyone out of here and on a ship back for Earth within the hour?" Tom asked him.

Jimmy nodded. "But I can't collect and move all the data," he pointed out. "I'd need—" He broke off and grinned wryly. "It no longer matters, does it? If the Sun goes nova, no one will ever need the information. And if you prevent the explosion, we can come back and retrieve the stuff in a safer way."

Tom bit his lip. Jimmy still had not given up hope! Neither had Tom. He had to come up with some idea to prevent this disaster!

"Better hurry," he said to Jimmy. "Leave us our ship, but take any other vessel capable of travel. You'll want to put as much distance between you and the Sun as possible."

The man nodded, then turned and left.

"What about him?" Anita Thorwald asked,

pointing at Dr. Wolfe, who, totally out of control now, was crying like a baby.

"He won't be any help to us. Why don't you and Ben take him back to the *Exedra*? And lock up David Luna on board, too. I don't like the idea of him running around loose and getting into trouble."

Ben escorted the industrialist from the room, while Anita gently led the whimpering scientist by the hand.

He followed her without any protest, wiping tears from his eyes.

"It's a shame seeing a man ruined mentally like that," Tom observed. "The strain of knowing deep down that he was responsible was just too much for him."

"He was a good researcher," Dr. Kerry added, "even though he had his faults, like being too stubborn and egotistical. But he deserves better than that. Luna really led him astray with his promises of fame and riches."

She ran another computer scan of the Sun's surface as Tom looked over her shoulder.

"Any change?" he asked.

"Not for the better. The null-space gate was actually sucking in parts of the Sun. It pulled up a pillar of hot gases halfway over to *SolarSat II*.

When we shut off the gateway, the column collapsed, but the damage was done."

"Is there any hope at all?"

"The excess energy is too massive. What we need is a way of draining it off without further disrupting the energy cycle. I don't see any way of doing that. We can't just open a hole in the center of the Sun and let it all leak off!"

Elizabeth heaved a deep sigh, then shivered even though the temperature inside the station was going up.

Suddenly, an idea grew in Tom's mind. He smiled.

Chapter Eighteen

"I've got it!" Tom exclaimed. "It's a really risky scheme, but we don't have anything to lose."

"What is it?" Elizabeth asked anxiously.

"The black hole I studied is nearing the Sun. It'll miss hitting it by several million miles, but maybe we can change the path."

"So what good does it do us having the black hole collide with the Sun?"

"It won't collide. The black hole is special in the universe. It's a tiny hole, smaller than a grain of sand. And it pulls in everything—and I mean *everything*—around it. Do you think it might be able to drain off all that excess energy that's making the Sun go nova?"

For a second, Dr. Kerry sat stunned. Then she said, "It might work. It might! We've got nothing to lose by trying it."

"This won't be easy," Tom cautioned. "That black hole is small, but massive. It'll take a lot of work to change its course and send it into the Sun."

"What will happen when it hits?" she asked, as she shut down the last of the instruments and began turning off power to all parts of *SolarSat II*. She wanted to take no chances on the null-space gateway opening again, even accidentally.

"That's the best part. The black hole is so massive, in spite of its size, it'll keep right on going. It'll pass through the Sun's center and leave the other side. Maybe by the time it's gone completely through, enough energy will have been absorbed to stop the explosion."

"Tom!" Ben stormed into the lab, with Anita right behind him. "Luna has locked himself in the *Exedra*. He got loose and ran ahead of us. We can't get him out."

"Oh, no!" Tom exclaimed. "We need that ship or all's lost!"

He turned on his heels and they all followed him through the now-deserted corridors of *SolarSat II*. Jimmy Nnamdi had already gotten the last of the research team into their ships and blasted off. Tom would have to get Luna to relent and allow them to board the *Exedra* if they wanted to escape themselves.

"Where's Aristotle?" He panted as he ran.

"I don't know," Ben replied. "He was talking with the station computer the last I saw him."

Tom raced to the nearest intercom, punched in the proper sequence of numbers, and connected to the *Exedra*'s control room. Through the hissing and crackling of static he heard David Luna's mocking voice.

"Now what are you going to do, Swift?" the evil industrialist taunted. "You can't enter your ship—and all the others have left. You might try to steal my idea but it won't do you any good."

"What are you proposing, Luna?"

"I want your cooperation. Unless you obey my commands, I'll keep you stranded on the station."

"Listen, Luna, that's my ship. It's fixed with a coding sequence that locks the controls. You're not going anywhere, either."

"I've noticed the computer-lock you put on it. That doesn't bother me. I've got all the time in the world."

"He still doesn't believe you, Tom," Ben hissed. "He thinks you're out to steal his invention."

"The computer-lock," Luna continued, "can be broken in time. As I said, I'm not the one in a hurry."

"We weren't lying, Luna. The Sun *is* going to

explode. We need the *Exedra* to reach that micro black hole and divert it."

The response was a harsh laugh.

"It's no good talking to him," Dr. Kerry said. "He won't listen."

"There's got to be some way in without destroying the hatch," Tom muttered.

Just then Aristotle walked up to them. "There is," he said. "I have spoken with the station computer. A biosensor monitors everyone aboard, for health reasons. Mister Luna has not slept in over thirty hours."

"So he's tired? So what?" Ben Walking Eagle impatiently paced back and forth in front of the lock hatch leading to the spaceship.

"I have taken the liberty of reducing the oxygen flow into the *Exedra*," the mechanoid explained. "As you know, decreased oxygen causes increased drowsiness in humans. He will not be harmed, but he will find it impossible to stay awake."

"That'll work!" Tom grinned. "He probably has an air quality monitor on to make sure we don't pump in sleeping gas. But he'll never notice a small decrease in oxygen content, because the instruments are set only for major malfunctions."

"What happens when he's asleep?" Ben demanded. "We wait for Rip Van Winkle to wake up again?"

"You are too impatient," Aristotle chided. "The station sensors report Mister Luna is now sound asleep. He is no longer in a position to block effort to open the hatch. His haste and unfamiliarity with our equipment has worked against him."

"It'll still take a cutting torch to open the airlock, and that'll destroy the ship!"

"No," the mechanoid corrected. "In conjunction with the station computer, I am transmitting instructions to the ship's onboard computer. Mister Luna neglected to turn it off before he conked out."

Ben could not help but laugh. "Aristotle, where'd you pick up such language?"

"From you," Aristotle said as the hatch mechanism began to churn and grind. In seconds, the airlock had opened.

"Tin man, you are a genius!" Tom congratulated his robot. "I'm so glad I invented you."

"I am pleased, too," the robot agreed.

The group rushed forward and found David Luna slumped across the control panel, snoring loudly. Ben and Aristotle shoved him into a back compartment with a strong lock on the door. The man barely stirred.

"Just in time, too," Tom said, checking the instruments. "A heavy solar flare is coming this way. Let's blast for the black hole. I've figured out a way it can save us."

Dr. Kerry acted as copilot again while the others performed preflight checks. In less than five minutes, Tom slammed down the switches and sent the *Exedra* blasting outward.

"It's good to be on the way, Tom," Elizabeth said as they moved away from *SolarSat II*. "But I'm still not clear on one thing."

"What's that?"

"How are we going to change the black hole's course?"

Tom looked sheepish. "I—don't know yet."

Chapter Nineteen

"What do you mean you don't know?" Anita demanded. "I thought you said you had it all figured out when you were talking back on the space station."

"I decided that getting the black hole to pass through the Sun's center is the way of preventing the explosion," Tom replied. "But one tiny detail remains unsolved."

Anita groaned. "How to move the black hole off its present course and onto the course we want."

"That's right."

"And here I thought we finally had it made."

"Have confidence, Anita," Aristotle spoke up.   155

"Tom has gotten us out of tight places before, if I understand the use of that particular idiom. I have faith in his ability to save the Solar System."

"Elizabeth, can you keep a close check on the Sun?" Tom asked. "I need a constant update. Ben, would you start a computer run to determine how big a force we're going to need to deflect the black hole once we get in its vicinity? Anita, Aristotle, go over the spaceship and make sure everything is in perfect working order. After passing so close to the Sun, lots of things might not work when we need them."

"And what are *you* going to do, Mister Swift?" Anita challenged.

"Think," came the simple reply.

"Sorry," the fiery redhead immediately apologized. "Of course that's what you've got to do." She flashed him a quick smile and turned to Aristotle, slapping him on one metallic side. "Come on, tin man, we've got a lot of work to do."

Aristotle pivoted on his motorframe, looking first at Anita, then at Tom, and finally back at Anita. His eyes flashed a bright green, as he obediently followed her into the depths of the ship.

Elizabeth furnished the young inventor a steady stream of information from her instruments, but it wasn't until Ben completed the computer analysis that an idea began to form in Tom's mind.

"It isn't a big change we have to make in the black hole's course," he said.

"A little nudge is all it'll take. Like Judo. A tiny force can produce a big result."

"A gravitational field might do it," Ben suggested.

"Gravity is the weakest of the cosmic forces," Tom objected. "It only appears strong because we see its effects all around us. The strongest is the nuclear force acting between particles inside an atom. That's what makes an atomic bomb so powerful—those forces are released within a few millionths of a second."

"So we set off an atomic bomb nearby. Will that do it?"

"We don't have an atomic bomb. Besides, it wouldn't do any good. The black hole would just suck up any energy in the vicinity. That ability is why we need it to pass through the Sun's core."

"So far, I haven't heard anything that sounds very useful to us," Ben said, helping Tom along by acting as a sounding board for ideas.

"Gravity is the weakest, but the next strongest are light, electricity, magnetism."

"I see a light dawning." Ben smiled. "The genius is getting ready to dazzle us all with a brilliant idea."

"I hope so," Dr. Kerry said in a low voice. "The Sun's activity is building drastically. It'll explode in less than three hours. My earlier estimates were wrong. Luna must have turned on the null-space gateway a lot sooner than we thought."

Tom Swift swung around in the contoured pilot's chair and faced his friends. A big smile crossed his face and his eyes danced with excitement.

"This is it! It's got to be!"

"So let us in on it," Ben urged.

"Gravity is out. There's no way we can manufacture enough, even with our artificial gravity generator, to really affect the black hole. Strong and weak nuclear forces are also out of our reach. But an electromagnetic one—in particular, a magnetic one—is possible."

"A strong enough magnetic field would affect the black hole," Dr. Kerry agreed with him. "But how are we ever going to generate a field big enough?"

"We turn the *Exedra* into a giant electromagnet. We send electricity through the hull, along wires wrapped around the entire ship. That'll do it. But everything will have to be very, very precise."

"I can see that," Elizabeth said, her excitement for the project now growing. "And the path the ship follows through space will have to be exactly right. The amount of current being fed into the wire wrappings will have to be controlled by the computer, too."

"But can it be done?" Ben asked.

"Yes!" both Tom and Dr. Kerry shouted in unison. They looked at one another, then laughed delightedly.

"Well, let's get a'cracking!" Ben exclaimed. "Just tell us what to do."

Tom started working with Anita and Aristotle on wrapping the outside of the ship in a cocoon of wire. When electricity was applied, a magnetic field strong enough to move the black hole would be created.

The young inventor left Anita and Aristotle to the task and went to check with Elizabeth and Ben.

"The Sun's not going to last much longer," the scientist said, worry wrinkling her forehead. "We've got less than two hours before it . . . it's all over." Her voice rose in pitch, then cracked under emotional strain.

"Tom won't let it happen," Ben said firmly. "His plan is going to work."

"And it's got to work the first time," Tom said. "The *Exedra* has to follow an exact course through space. This will give the maximum magnetic field at precisely the instant it's needed most. If we miss, I'd have to turn the *Exedra* around and come back—and that would take days."

"First time or nothing," Anita said, entering the control room. "If anyone in the Solar System can do it, it's you, Tom."

The young inventor almost blushed with the confidence his friends showed in him.

"Let's make sure all the data is put into the computer."

"What is most important, Tom?" Ben asked.

"The ship's velocity," he answered quickly. "The magnet has to be turned on at exactly the right instant. Our speed and direction will make the black hole 'twitch' and go off at an angle. That angle has to be one that sends it into the Sun."

Ben was soon lost in a sea of numbers. His nimble fingers worked on the keyboard until all lights flashed green.

"Aristotle is about finished wiring up the ship's hull," Anita said. "We had to pirate almost every instrument and electrical appliance on the ship."

"You didn't take the power cord off my personal computer?" Ben asked suspiciously. "I'm using that to work on the names for the soda pop contest."

"I most certainly did take its power cord," Anita said.

Ben glared at her.

"We needed the electrical wire," she explained. Then a wicked look came into her sparkling green eyes. "Besides, that computer was putting you ahead of me. Now we'll both have to use our heads."

"We do?" Ben blurted. "I bet you have your own computer working on this!"

"Well, I don't need it to run my leg all the time," the redhead admitted. She glanced down to where her bionic leg emerged from her jumpsuit, then patted it. A tiny humming indicated that she did have it working on the problem of going through millions of possible names.

"No fair!" Ben cried. "You'll—"

Tom interrupted their playful banter by turning to Elizabeth. "I don't think either one of them cares about winning the contest. They don't even know what the first prize is. They're more interested in beating each other. Either would be happy to finish next to last as long as the other was last."

Dr. Kerry laughed. The rivalry was a friendly one and it took their minds off their serious mission. But only for a moment.

Suddenly red lights flashed on the console. Tom checked the radar display and said, "The black hole is exactly in position. It's a good thing I researched it earlier, otherwise we wouldn't have found it this easily. We're almost right on target."

"I'm changing course slightly," Dr. Kerry decided. "We need to line up a bit more precisely."

The *Exedra* shivered as tiny fingers of rocket blast altered its course just the right amount. Only when they were in perfect alignment did Tom turn to Anita and ask, "Are the coils ready to be turned on?"

"All set, Tom. This entire ship's going to be the strongest magnet ever seen in this part of space. It'll even pull the iron out of your blood."

"No magnet is that powerful, Anita," Aristotle lectured. "In fact, there is no magnetic field at all in the center of the magnet's wire windings. Maxwell's equations dealing with electromagnetism explain why we will not experience any such attraction or repulsion."

Tom looked at the ceiling and rolled his eyes. While Aristotle understood exaggeration and jokes, he sometimes didn't know when his friends were using them to lighten the mood.

"Last check before starting," the young inventor said.

"The Sun's activity is growing more critical by the second," Dr. Kerry told him.

"Ship's mass and thrust are constant," Ben said.

"Electromagnet ready for use," Aristotle reported.

"Then let's do it." Tom watched as the course was shown on a visual display. The black hole was represented by a tiny dot. The *Exedra* showed as a moving green line. At the far corner of the screen was a curving bright yellow line—the Sun.

The green line moved forward, on a course that would cause it to pass parallel to the black hole.

Tom felt the tension mounting. When a loud clank echoed from the aft section of the *Exedra*, he jumped a foot.

"What was that?" he cried. "Aristotle, check on it right away. We can't have anything going wrong now."

"I will see what has occurred." The mechanoid swung on his motorframe and whirred off to correct whatever had come loose.

Tom studied the instruments but everything was still perfect. But a cold chill ran up and down his spine when Aristotle called for him a moment later. He ran to the rear.

"Tom," the robot said, "I failed to anticipate Mister Luna's ingenuity."

"What do you mean?" Tom glanced at the electronic lock on the storeroom, where Luna had been held captive. Then he saw it. The man had succeeded in short-circuiting it and was now loose aboard the *Exedra*!

"This couldn't have happened at a worse time," he murmured. "Find him as fast as you can, Aristotle. Find him and keep him from sabotaging the mission."

Aristotle left to search for Luna and Tom joined the others again when a huge shudder wracked the *Exedra*. Tom was thrown to one side. Only his quick reflexes kept him from injury.

"What was that?" Ben shouted. "It's thrown us off course. The mass of the ship has changed, too. We are several hundred kilograms lighter. What's going on?"

Tom shook his head. Everywhere he looked, red warning lights flashed on and off.

Just then Aristotle walked in. "I have bad news," he said.

"Yes?" Tom felt his stomach tighten.

"David Luna has taken the starboard escape nodule and left!"

"The lifeboat!" Tom exclaimed. "That's about the worst thing that could have happened. When he jetted off, he changed our course."

"Is there time to correct it?" Anita asked anxiously.

"No," the young inventor said in a choked voice. "We'll have to do the best we can, though. Ben, give me full computer control. Elizabeth, forget about monitoring the Sun. I need you as copilot. Anita, make sure that Luna left without planting a bomb on board or doing some other kind of damage."

On the display screen, the tiny green line indicated the *Exedra* veered to one side. A new spot of light, a green circle, traveled at right angles. This was the lifeboat David Luna had stolen.

"We don't have enough time or thrust to get back on course," Tom finally said. "So we'll have to do this by the seat of our pants. The computer is giving me IMPOSSIBLE readings. It'll shut down if its calculations show we can't make it."

He took over manual control of the *Exedra*. Anita poised near the switch that would send electricity running through the coil circling the ship. The others watched in tense, nervous anticipation.

The green line changed direction slightly, moving them back almost along the course they'd had before Luna left.

"It's not close enough, Tom," Dr. Kerry cried.

"It has to be." Tom's determination would make it right. They didn't dare fail!

"The computer locked up, just as you thought, Tom," Ben reported. "I turned it off."

Tom nodded. "Now, Anita, put the juice to the coils."

Lights inside the ship flickered as all available

energy went through the huge electromagnet.

Tom watched the display screen for a clue as to their success or failure. For the span of several rapid heartbeats, nothing appeared to happen.

"It's moving, Tom! You've done it!" Ben shouted suddenly. "Look at the way the black hole is changing direction!"

Chapter Twenty

Tom sagged back. "It's not going where I wanted it to!" he cried out. "The black hole isn't on a direct collision course with the Sun."

"But it will pass through it," Doctor Kerry assured him. "I've run a check on the course. It'll be close enough."

"I hope you're right," Ben said.

Tom watched the display screen, his stomach knotted with tension and anticipation. The dot representing the black hole moved slowly toward the yellow curve of the Sun. Off to one side, almost leaving the screen, traveled the green circle that had cause the mission so much trouble.

"One thing's for sure," Ben said. "If David 167

Luna made us miss, he won't be able to escape, either."

"Some consolation," Anita muttered. She rested her hands on Tom's shoulders. "How long will it be before we know if it worked?"

"Only a few more minutes," the young inventor said. His eyes never wavered from their scrutiny of the screen. "If only Luna hadn't used the emergency nodule when he had! If he'd waited only a little while longer!"

Dr. Kerry held up a hand. "The Sun's activity is changing pattern!" she said excitedly. "The black hole is finally getting close enough to have a real effect!"

"Is it sufficient?" Tom asked.

"There's no way of telling. Not yet. It'll have to pass all the way through the Sun before we know that." She paused a moment, then went on, her voice almost cracking with emotion. "Now it's inside the photosphere. It's going on in! Going down—hitting the Sun's surface!" She sucked in her breath and held it. Only after a long minute did she exhale noisily. "It's inside. And the energy level is dropping."

"Is it dropping enough?" Anita was pale with tension.

"Wait. The results are coming in now. While the energy level hasn't decreased as much as we'd originally calculated for a direct hit, it's sufficient.

Tom, you've saved everyone in the Solar System from a fiery death!"

"Oh, Tom!" Anita squealed. She grabbed him around the neck and almost smothered him. The blond inventor smiled and let out a sigh of relief. Then he became serious again.

"It's not over. Even if the Sun doesn't go nova, there might be problems from this in the future. David Luna might have upset the Sun's cycle so badly that other measures will have to be taken."

"I don't think so," Elizabeth Kerry said. "The Sun is pretty stable as stars go. Even if what you're saying is true, it'd be hundreds or thousands of years in the future."

"We need to study the Sun more," he declared. "Accidents like this should never happen."

"That's why I'm devoting my life to solar research," the pretty blonde scientist said. "I don't ever want to think we don't know about something so vital to all our lives."

"Great," Ben spoke up. "And now I want to go home. Let's head back for *New America*. I've got a contest to win!"

"Says you!" Anita retorted.

"Tom," cut in Aristotle, "are you going to abandon Mister Luna? We are a considerable distance away from any human habitation. The life support capabilities of the emergency nodule are limited."

"You're right. We ought to find him, scoop him up, and take him back. I want him to stand trial for all he's done."

"There is a problem with that," Aristotle cautioned. "Technically, at least in the eyes of the law, Mister Luna has committed no crime."

"What do you mean?" Anita flared. "He tried to murder everyone in the entire Solar System!"

"That would be very difficult to prove. We know it is the likely result of his experiment. However, a judge and jury might see it differently."

"Aristotle's right," Tom said slowly. "*We* know what Luna's done. Getting anyone else to believe it is almost impossible."

"Doctor Wolfe can give testimony!"

"Doctor Wolfe is disturbed emotionally. I don't believe anyone would take him seriously. But Luna might be paying a bigger price than he knows," Tom added, checking his scanner. "I've lost contact with the lifeboat."

"If we do not pick him up, Tom, he cannot reach either the Moon base or Earth. He will be stranded without oxygen and die," Aristotle stated matter-of-factly.

"He's nowhere to be seen on the radar," Ben spoke up, after running a computer scan.

"So we search," Tom declared.

But David Luna wasn't to be found.

Ben stretched out on a grassy knoll where he and his friends had spread a cloth for a picnic, to which they had invited Woody Bragg, the pilot of the *Ponderous*. He had recovered his health after extensive treatment and was forever grateful to Tom for saving his life.

"That was some adventure you had," he said after hearing the details of their trip.

"It was," Ben admitted. "But I tell you, *New America* never looked so good to me. The stale air aboard the *Exedra* is nothing compared to this!"

Bees hummed, flowers bloomed in wild profusion, and the air was fresh with the smell of springtime. The gentle curve of the inside of the space colony made the landscape look strange, but none of them minded. They'd grown used to seeing the horizon stretch up and vanish into clouds overhead. Even the view of a lake bending along the curvature didn't surprise them.

"Things have definitely worked out for the best," Tom said. "The Sun is back in its familiar stable pattern. We aren't even getting those solar flares now."

"I explained all that happened to Doctor Connors," Elizabeth spoke up. "It took some doing, but he finally agreed he'd been reading his data wrong and that you hadn't caused those flares by studying the black hole."

"Bet he didn't believe David Luna had been the

culprit, though," Anita said. "It does seem far-fetched that a null-space gateway could do so much damage."

"He believed," Dr. Kerry said, "but it was a reluctant belief. Manfred Wolfe gave the final proof."

"How is Doctor Wolfe?" asked Tom. "Has he recovered?"

"Once the strain was off, his condition improved a great deal. He'll never work in research again, though. Everyone in the scientific community knows how dangerous his experiments really were."

"I want to know what happened to that snake Luna." Anita rolled over and popped a stuffed olive into her mouth. She bit down hard—as if she could take her ire out on it.

"He's never been found. No report of the life-ship has come in, either."

"He died, then," Ben said.

"I can't say for sure." Tom shrugged. "David Luna is a wily man, very smart, very resourceful. If anyone could survive, it's he."

"Let's not talk about such unpleasant things," Ben piped up. "This is a celebration. We have just saved all of humankind and we deserve to enjoy ourselves."

"Agreed!" They lifted plastic cans and drank.

Then, as one, they sputtered and spat out the contents.

"Ben, what *is* this stuff? It's awful!" Anita cried.

Ben looked sheepish. "This is Cosmo Pop. I bought a case of it to see if I couldn't get some inspiration."

"Cosmo Pop?"

"My name—the one that's going to win."

"How many names did you send in?"

"Four hundred, but Cosmo Pop's the one I like best. It's sure to win."

"The name may be a winner, but this stuff isn't. Anita put the soda down, obviously wanting to pour it onto the grass but worrying that it might kill anything it touched.

"Hello!" Aristotle called from the foot of the hill. "I am bringing good news."

A man carrying a large box was accompanying the robot. They quickly climbed the steep hill and approached the picnickers.

"This is Mr. Horvath of Consolidated Earth Beverages," Aristotle explained. "He is the contest director and has a surprise for you."

"Yes, indeed I do," the man spoke up. "I understand one of you is Benjamin Franklin Walking Eagle?"

All eyes turned to Ben.

"I am," he said.

Mr. Horvath nodded. "It is my privilege to award you second prize in the soda pop contest."

"Second? Well, it's better than nothing." Ben took an envelope the man handed him. "Who won first prize?"

"I, uh, this is very difficult. When I contacted, uh, him, it took me by surprise. I had to get a ruling from the board of directors."

"Why?" Ben asked.

"Because the winner isn't human."

Silence fell until Aristotle made a small whirring sound.

"I am the winner," the mechanoid spoke up.

"You?" Ben exclaimed. "What was your winning name?"

"He proved very imaginative," Mr. Horvath said, "giving us both a name and a slogan. 'SunBeam—it goes nova in your mouth.' Great, isn't it? And first prize is certainly well deserved. Here it is, Aristotle."

Aristotle took the large box the man had carried and unpacked it. Inside was a foot-high robot!

"Oh—I—" he sputtered.

"It's one of the most advanced mechanoids of that size available on the market," Mr. Horvath explained. "Uh, it's nothing like you, I'm sure, but it can be programmed to do simple tasks." He nodded, then left quickly.

The little robot clanked and lurched when turned on. For a moment it tottered, then looked at Aristotle. It bumped gently into his motorframe, then stopped. Anita and Elizabeth broke out in gales of laughter.

"I think our tin man has a family now, even if the offspring is a bit on the simple side," Ben exclaimed. "What are you going to call him—Junior?" He chuckled at Aristotle's obvious uneasiness with his prize.

"Ben, you haven't examined the envelope yet," Aristotle said. "It contains your prize."

"Yes, go on!" Tom urged. "Let's see what you've won and if it matches Aristotle's fabulous present."

Ben ripped open the envelope and took out a piece of paper while Tom looked over his shoulder. Then he groaned. "I knew it!" he said in disgust. "Something like this was bound to happen. Second prize is a free mail order course in computer programming. Just what I need!"

The friends doubled over with laughter. Everything seemed relaxed now but soon they'd be involved in a new and exciting adventure, *Tom Swift: The Invisible Force.*

"Let's finish eating," Ben suggested. "Then we can watch the sunset."

Anita nodded. "I never realized just how special that is until now!"

THE TOM SWIFT ® SERIES
by Victor Appleton

You will also enjoy

THE HARDY BOYS ® SERIES
by Franklin W. Dixon